Uneasy Lies the Dead

KENDELL FOSTER CROSSEN
Writing as
M.E. CHABER

STEEGER BOOKS / **2020**

PUBLISHED BY STEEGER BOOKS
Visit steegerbooks.com for more books like this.

PUBLISHING HISTORY

Hardcover
New York: Holt, Rinehart & Winston, January 1964. Dust jacket by Ben Feder, Inc.
Toronto: Holt, Rinehart & Winston of Canada, 1964.
London: T. V. Boardman (American Bloodhound Mystery #470), 1964.

Paperback
New York: Paperback Library (63-328), A Milo March Mystery, #8, May 1970. Cover by Robert McGinnis.

ISBN: 978-1-61827-529-5

For the one and only—Lisa

CONTENTS

ONE

It was a nice little club on Euclid Avenue in Cleveland, Ohio. You know the kind—with dim lights, fancy furnishings, and stiff prices. The attraction, as far as I was concerned, was a blues singer named Lola Crane. She was about five feet seven and a hundred and twenty pounds. Every pound of it was in just the right place. Her hair was honey-colored. She had the kind of voice that makes your throat tighten up when you hear it. I'd discovered her by accident the second night I was in Cleveland. I'd been back several times, but this was the first night I could relax and really enjoy it.

The name's March. Milo March. I'm an insurance investigator with my own office in New York. I'd been in Cleveland a week, working for the Security Insurance Company. It was a small outfit that gave me a job maybe once a year. This time it had been some broad who had killed her husband and thought she was going to collect his insurance.

She might have gotten away with it, too, if she'd been a little more patient. He had been listed on the police files as a victim of a hit-and-run accident. That meant the company paid double. They resigned themselves to their fate and were about to pay off. Then, about two weeks after the accident, a clerk for the insurance company drove down her street on his way home from a night out with the boys. It was three o'clock in the morning. It just happened that he was the clerk who was processing her claim. It also happened that he was ambitious. So he noticed the lights on in her house and thought he saw a couple dancing in the living room. He didn't think that was the way for a brand-new widow to act, so the next morning he reported it.

The company didn't get excited, but they asked a few questions. The widow said there wasn't any party; it was just that she was so upset she had to call her doctor. He verified that he'd been there and said he'd had to give her a sedative. The only thing that bothered the company, after they thought about it for a while, was that he was the same doctor who had signed the death certificate. They got a court order and had the body dug up and an autopsy performed. The husband had been killed by a car, all right—he'd been run over three or four times—but he was also full of enough morphine to have kept him unconscious for a week. The company called me.

It had taken me a week to wrap the case up, and the doctor and the lovely widow were both locked up. The company was so grateful they gave me a thousand dollars over my fee of seven hundred. That had made me so grateful that I decided to spend part of it in Cleveland before catching the plane the next morning. So there I was at the Hideout, drinking V.O. at a buck and a half a shot and letting Lola Crane's voice send shivers up and down my spine.

She was just finishing her final number when I beckoned the waiter.

He hurried over. "Another one, sir?" he asked, reaching for my glass, which was still half full.

"In a moment," I said. "Ask Miss Crane if she'll join me for a drink."

He shook his head. "I don't think she will, sir. She doesn't do that sort of thing."

"Why don't you ask her and find out," I suggested. I slid a five-dollar bill across the table.

He hesitated a second, then scooped it up. He turned and went to meet her.

I was pretty sure she'd come. It wasn't that I thought I was irresistible; I was sure that curiosity would get to her. I had sat at that same table alone every night I'd been in Cleveland. It was near enough to the small stage so that she couldn't have helped seeing me.

I'd been right. She listened to the waiter and then came directly to my table. I got to my feet.

"I'm glad you came, Miss Crane," I said. "I wanted to tell you how much I've enjoyed your singing. Won't you join me for a drink?"

"Thank you," she said.

I went around and held the chair for her. She sat down and I suddenly found myself looking down over her shoulder. It was a lovely view. It answered one thing I'd been wondering. Only nature had ever made anything like them.

I couldn't think of an excuse for lingering, so I went back to my chair. "My name is Milo March," I said.

"Hello," she said with a smile.

The waiter came over and I looked at her.

"Bourbon and water," she said.

I ordered it for her and another V.O. for myself. Then I

turned back to her.

"You've been here almost every night for a week," she said. "Why?"

"I've told you. I think you're one of the most exciting singers I've heard in a long time."

"That's very nice to hear, but I've been here for two months. How come it took you so long to discover me?"

"I'm from New York. I just arrived in Cleveland a week ago. I happened to wander in here the first night and liked what I heard—and saw. So I've come back. I'm leaving tomorrow, and I thought I'd tell you how much I liked your singing before I left."

The waiter arrived with the drinks.

"Too bad you're not a talent scout," she said with a smile. "I could use a little discovering. But it's sweet of you to tell me anyway. Thank you."

"To your being discovered," I said solemnly, lifting my drink.

We drank to that and I looked her over again. She moved a little but it was with pleasure not embarrassment. And when I glanced at her face, there was amusement in her eyes as well as enjoyment.

"You have another show, don't you?" I asked.

She nodded. "I can't stay long because of that. I go on again in an hour, and I have to change and rest a few minutes."

"Sure," I said. "Maybe we can have another drink when you're through."

She gave me a long look from beneath her lashes. "Maybe," she said. She finished her drink and stood up. "Thank you, Mr. March."

"It was my pleasure," I said. It was, too, especially when she turned and started to walk away. I watched until I lost her in the darker recesses of the club. Then I sat down and went back to my drink. It didn't taste nearly as good as it had before.

I had almost finished it when I was aware that somebody was standing beside my table. I looked up. He was dressed like a waiter, but he certainly wasn't one. His dinner jacket was bulging at the seams, especially under the left arm. His face looked as if he'd spent most of his life as a sparring partner for Sonny Liston.

"You," he said, "the boss wants to see you."

"Fine," I said. "Send him over."

"Nah. In the office." He jerked his head toward the rear of the club.

"Who's the boss?"

"You'll see. You want to walk back or you want to be carried back?"

"Depends on who does the carrying. You're not my type." I stood up. "What's the idea of all the strong-arm stuff?"

"The boss said he wanted to see you. What the boss says goes—one way or another. Start walking."

We threaded our way back through the tables. At the rear of the room there were a few steps going up to another level. When I reached the top, there were two ways to go, so I stopped.

"Left," he said.

I turned left and that brought me up in front of a door, a good strong door by the looks of it.

"Open the door and go in," he said.

"Wouldn't it be more polite to knock first?" I asked.

"Don't be smart. Open the door and walk in." He gave me a shove that almost removed the necessity of opening the door.

I filed it away in my memory and turned the knob. The door swung open and I walked into an office—some office. Everything was in white, the big thick rug, the walls and draperies, the desk and chairs, even the telephone. There was a man sitting at the desk, a well-built man with gray hair. He was also wearing a dinner coat, but his fitted him. He was smooth, a little too smooth.

"Here he is, boss," the one behind me said.

Then I noticed something else. Directly in front of the desk was a large window. Through it you could see the entire floor of the nightclub and everything that went on. But, I remembered, when you looked up from the floor, what you saw was a big section of what seemed to be a mural on frosted glass. It was one-way glass.

"I can see him," the man said. "Get outside, Rocks. I'll call you when I want you." He sounded as smooth as he looked. He waited until the door closed behind me.

"Sit down," he said then.

"An invitation or an order?" I asked.

"Take it any way you like," he said. "Stand up if it makes you feel bigger."

So I sat down in the chair beside his desk, facing him. I pointed a thumb in the direction of the one-way glass. "Nice view you have there."

"I like it." He was looking me over as if I were a new piece of furniture he'd ordered for the office.

"Look," I said, before he could start, "I gather you have some sort of speech to make to me. Before you start, I have one of my own. If you ever want to see me again, send me a nice invitation, not some goon who starts giving me orders. And especially a goon who shoves me. I don't like it. Now, who the hell are you?"

"I'm Nick Potti." He said it the same way that the President of the United States might announce that his name was Johnson. But it didn't mean a thing to me.

"A nice name," I said. "What am I supposed to do? Ask for your autograph, swoon, or just scream a little?"

"Very funny," he said. "You're Milo March, an insurance dick."

"Gee, that's pretty good. You want to try for the mink coat by telling me how many dimples I have? Or do you have a swami hidden behind the bar who reads the drops of whiskey left in each glass?"

"This is the fifth night you been here," he said. "Each night you sat at the same table—alone. This ain't the kind of club where a guy comes alone. I notice things like that."

"That's nice," I said. "Do you always go around picking up guys who are alone? If so, I'm sorry to disappoint you. I like girls."

That time I got to him. A little red crept into his cheeks.

"Don't be so smart you blow your own brains out," he snapped. "I want to know what the hell you're doing here."

"Enjoying myself—up until now. I stopped in the first night and thought you had a hell of a good singer. So I came back."

"I noticed. You were talking to her, too. What about?"

"I told you. I like girls. And I like girl singers. Is it against the law for a man to talk to a girl in this town?"

"That's all?"

"I might have other ideas about her besides talking," I admitted, "but that's strictly between the girl and me. It's not any of your business."

"I might make it my business."

"Not you," I said. "You wouldn't like it. There's no cash in it. Just a man and a woman. Like the birds and the bees, although probably no one ever told you about them either."

His face darkened again. "It wouldn't take much to make me dislike you, March."

"I'm not so fond of you either," I said. "You could have saved both of us from all of this by just leaving me where I was. And I still don't know what the hell this is all about."

He had himself under control again. "I told you. This ain't a place where a guy comes in and sits by himself. If he does once, then he don't come back. When I noticed you out there for the third night in a row, I started to find out about you. So you're Milo March, an insurance dick from New York. And I still want to know why you're here five nights this week."

"I told you. The singer."

"You come all the way from New York just to see a broad?"

I looked at him and laughed. "Now I get it. You have cop fever."

"Cops don't bother me," he snapped. "I'm clean."

"I'll bet," I said. "Well, relax, Potti. I came out here a week ago to work on a case for an insurance company. A broad bumped off her ever-loving. I finished the case today, and I was planning on going back to New York tomorrow—unless you get me so interested I decide I'd like to work for nothing."

He stared at me for a minute. "All right," he said. He reached under his desk with one hand. I didn't hear anything, but the door opened and the big guy looked in.

"Yeah, boss?"

"Take Mr. March back to his table and tell Emil his check is on the house for tonight."

"Don't do me any favors," I said, starting for the door. "I can pay my own way."

"You heard me, Rocks," he said flatly. "And, March ... ?"

"Yes?"

"Stay away from my singer."

"Oh?" I said. "Do you own her, too?"

"You heard what I said. Stay away from her."

"I heard you—and I'm beginning to get very interested." I stepped through the door past the big fellow. "Come on, Valentino. Escort me back to my table."

We went back the way we'd come, me in front and him right behind me. We reached my table and I sat down.

"That was very sweet of you," I told him. "Now run along like a good boy. I'm already promised for the next dance."

He scowled at me, but he left without saying anything. He stopped to talk to the waiter for a minute and then disappeared toward the back. The waiter came over at once.

"What would you like, sir?" he asked.

"About an inch of jugular vein, but I'll settle for a double V.O."

"Yes, sir," he said and scurried away.

I was still fuming a half hour later when Lola Crane came back to sing again. But as I listened to her voice—and looked at what it was coming from—I relaxed and began to forget about my anger. When she did her last song, I got up and walked over to meet her as she came off the stage.

"That was great, honey," I said.

"Why, thank you, Mr. March."

"Still feel like joining me for that drink?"

"Uh-huh. Just as soon as I change."

"Tell me one thing first," I said. "Who's this Nick Potti?"

She stared at me for a full minute. "You really don't know?"

"Never heard of him in my life."

"That's because you're not from Cleveland," she said slowly. "He's a big man around here."

"Just because he owns this club?"

"No, not because of that. He—he does a lot of things, I guess."

"You mean he's a big man in the rackets?"

"That's what a lot of people say," she told me. "Why?"

"Do you belong to him?"

"I do not," she said indignantly. "If you think that I "

"Hold it," I said, taking her hand. "I only asked you that because he told me to stay away from you."

"He told you that? When?"

"While you were in your dressing room."

Her face twisted into a crooked smile. "So now you're trying to tell me that you suddenly remembered that you had something else to do tonight?"

"Not at all. I thought maybe you'd want to change your mind."

"He doesn't tell me what to do."

"Okay, then, honey. It's a date. Go change your clothes. I'll be " Somebody tapped me on the shoulder. I looked around. It was the big gorilla again.

"The boss told you to stay away from the broad," he said.

"Get out of here, Rocks," the girl said angrily.

"I'll take care of it, honey," I said. I looked at him. "You heard the lady. Go play with your marbles—if you have any left."

The scowl bit deeper into his forehead.

Just then I heard a voice calling from the bar. "Emil," it said, "see if there's a Mr. March in the place. Somebody wants him on the phone."

I half turned and waved to the bartender. "That's for me," I said. "I'll be right there."

That was when he hit me. Fortunately it was a little high, catching me on the cheek, or I might have been out like a shorted light. As it was, I stumbled back a few steps, then hit the floor. My head was ringing. I shook it and got slowly to my feet. The orchestra had suddenly started playing louder.

"I should have known that was about your speed," I told Rocks. "Why don't you hit me when I'm looking at you? What color's that stripe on your back—yellow or lavender?"

He made a sound deep in his throat and rushed me, which was what I wanted. I stepped to one side and planted a hard right in his ribs as he went by. I heard him grunt and knew I'd hurt him. He staggered and almost went down. He was trying to regain his balance when I moved in. I decided this was no time for politeness. I kicked him as hard as I could right on the left kneecap. He groaned and half bent over with pain. I straightened him up with a right to the nose, spun him partly around with a left, and put my right to the corner of his chin as hard as I could. His face went blank and he folded to the floor like an old balloon.

"That was on me," I said. I looked at the girl, who was still standing there, her hand to her mouth. "Run along and change, honey. I'll be waiting for you."

She nodded and fled toward the rear of the room. I stepped over the body on the floor and went to the bar. The bartender was standing there with his mouth hanging open.

"I'm Mr. March," I said. "I'll take that phone call."

"Yes, sir," he said uncertainly. "You can take it in that private booth over there, if you wish, sir. It's an extension of this phone."

"Thanks," I said. I walked over to the booth, stepped in, and closed the door. I wondered who could be calling me. I hadn't told anyone at the hotel where I was going when I left. I picked up the receiver and said hello.

"Mr. Milo March?" the voice asked. It was obviously an operator.

"Speaking," I said. "But just a minute, operator. I'd prefer to wait until the extension phone is hung up." There was a loud sound as the bartender slammed down the receiver. "All right, operator."

"New York is calling. Just a minute, please."

There was the sound of several operators talking back and forth to each other across the country, and finally another voice came on. I recognized it the minute I heard it.

"Milo, boy, how are you?" he asked. It was Martin Raymond, vice-president of Intercontinental Insurance Company.

"I was fine until now," I said. "Do you know what time it is?"

"Sure," he said cheerfully. "I've been trying to get you since six o'clock."

"Persistent, aren't you? How did you find me?"

"Easy. When you hadn't been back to your hotel by eight o'clock, I called Ernie Tallmer at Security. Your phone service told me you were working for them. Ernie told me you finished up their case today. So I knew where you'd be. I just had the operator start through the Cleveland phone book calling every bar and nightclub and asking for you. That's all there was to it."

"Okay, Sherlock," I said.

"Congratulations on the job you did for Security. Ernie was very happy about it."

"He ought to be. It saved him about two hundred thousand dollars. Is that all you called me up for?"

"No. We have a little job for you."

"I'll be back in New York tomorrow. You can tell me about it then."

"As a matter of fact, Milo, the case is partly in Cleveland. That's why I wanted to catch you before you left."

I sighed. "All right. What is it?"

"It's too big to tell you on the phone. This is a really big one, Milo, boy. We have a branch office in Cleveland. Drop around there tomorrow and they'll give you the whole story. See Frank Hudson. He's got all the details. Don't fail us on this one, Milo. It's a big one."

"You make it sound like somebody stole Lake Erie. The usual fee?"

"Sure. A hundred a day and expenses. I've already instructed Hudson to give you some expense money. And Milo ..." His voice dropped to a confidential tone.

"Yes?"

"I think I can promise you a healthy bonus on this one if you deliver for us."

"I always like to hear you say that, Martin—the gritted teeth, the strained voice, the tear in the eye."

"Good old Milo. Anything for a laugh, eh, kid? Have a good time."

"I intend to," I said.

I hung up and left the booth. The body was gone from the floor and I didn't see it around anywhere. I went over to the bar and had another drink while I waited.

She came in just as I was finishing my drink. She looked just as good in street clothes as she did in the evening dress.

"Hi," I said as she came up. "Did I remember to tell you that you're beautiful?"

"No," she said. She smiled wanly, looking frightened. "Where's Rocks?"

"I don't know. The body was gone when I came back from taking my phone call. Don't worry about it."

"All right," she said, but I noticed that she glanced nervously over her shoulder.

"I'll tell you what, honey. Let's go somewhere else and have our drink."

"All right," she said quickly.

I paid the bartender, tipped him and the waiter, and we left. We stopped under the canopy outside. There were several taxis at a stand to our left. I motioned for one. "Where shall we go?" I asked. "It's your town."

"Well," she said, "most of the places are probably already closed. The others will be closing within an hour. I have a bar in my apartment. Why don't we go there?"

"Best offer I've had all day," I said solemnly as I helped her into the taxi.

TWO

I was up early the next morning and had a quick breakfast in the hotel. I had a couple of small drinks for the benefit of my hangover and then went over to the Intercontinental offices on Superior Avenue. I told them who I was, and I was ushered right into Mr. Hudson's office.

He was a road-company version of Martin Raymond. He was wearing a Brooks Brothers suit, or a reasonable facsimile. He had the handshake of the young executive who knows damn well who's going to salute the flag when he runs it up the pole. Martin Raymond must have given me quite a buildup to him because he was impressed even though he was trying to suppress it.

"Well, it's a pleasure to have you here," he said. "Martin was telling me how much good work you've done for the company. And I've read some of the reports, of course."

The last sentence was thrown in to show me that he was important, too. He'd probably never even heard of one of my reports before.

"Of course," I said solemnly. "Martin said that you'd give me the details on the case."

"Glad to. We have a file on it which you can look at. Personally, I think it's a lost cause."

"Why?"

"Remember the name Thomas Rako?"

I dredged something up out of my memory. "He was a gangster, a little one. Somebody bumped him off a few years ago, or something of the sort."

"Close enough," he said. "Rako had a record. But he was more than a gangster. He was the business manager of the Carrier Workers Union of America here in Cleveland. He was called up before a Congressional committee a few years ago and took the Fifth. The next day he vanished. Some people thought he was killed, some had other ideas."

"I remember now," I said. "The Carrier Workers and Johnny Clark. He's the guy who set out to buck the Teamsters and swore he was going to make Jimmy Hoffa* look like a bum."

"Well, he didn't quite do that, but he did pretty well. He's taken a lot of locals away from the Teamsters. Then he has the one local that covers every kind of job you can think of because all of them need some sort of transportation. That local has its headquarters here in Cleveland, and Thomas Rako was the head of it until he vanished."

"What does it have to do with us?" I had an uneasy feeling. "Don't tell me that Intercontinental carried insurance on Rako."

"That's it," he said. "Two policies: one in which his wife was the beneficiary and another in which the beneficiary was the Rack Trucking Company here in Cleveland."

---

* Jimmy Hoffa was a powerful labor leader who was president of the teamsters' union and also had links to organized crime. Tried for jury tampering and other crimes, he was convicted around the time of this publication (1964). In a strange echo of the Thomas Rako character, Hoffa mysteriously disappeared in 1975; he was never found. (All footnotes were added by the editor.)

"Tell me the rest of the bad news," I said.

"Rako disappeared six years and eleven months ago. Nothing has been heard about him since. In thirty more days the courts can declare him legally dead, and Intercontinental will have to pay up."

"How much?"

"One million dollars. Each policy is for a half million."

"Good old Martin Raymond," I said. "I should have known that he wouldn't spend half the night trying to get me unless it was something like that. Who owns the trucking company that's the beneficiary in one policy? Rako?"

"Mrs. Grace Rako and Mrs. Helen Clark. She's the wife of the President of the Carrier Workers."

I was remembering more. The Congressional hearings were held because the committee claimed that Johnny Clark had used union money to set up the trucking firm which was owned by his wife and Thomas Rako's. It was Rako who was the key witness, and he had disappeared.

"I don't suppose," I said, "anyone's been looking for Rako since he did the vanishing act?"

"Oh, yes," Hudson said cheerfully. "I believe the police of several cities have been active, and so have the men of the Federal Bureau of Investigation."

"Great. They've been looking for him for six years and eleven months without any success, and now I'm supposed to find him in thirty days."

"Mr. Raymond has great confidence in you," he said.

I had the feeling, however, that he was secretly hoping that Martin Raymond and I would both fall flat on our faces.

I uttered a short word that's usually reserved for locker rooms. "Sure, he wants miracles for a hundred dollars a day. Okay, where's the file?"

Hudson called his secretary, who brought me the file and led me to an unoccupied office where I could look at it. There wasn't much more in it than he'd told me. And the only thing on the disappearance was a batch of newspaper clippings. Finally I carried the whole file back to Hudson.

"I gather you don't have to employ very many file clerks," I told him, "if this is an example of your files."

"What's wrong with it?" he asked. "That's all we have."

"So I noticed. Tell me, has the insurance company done anything in the last six years about finding Rako?"

"Well … no. You see, the committee found him guilty of contempt, and we thought he was just trying to dodge it and would show up sooner or later."

"Trusting little souls, aren't you?" I observed. "If a guy wants to insure his furniture for five hundred bucks, you suspect him of being an arsonist, but if a guy stands to collect a million dollars you think he's going to show up. Thanks for all the help. In the meantime, I believe that something was said about my drawing some expense money from you."

"Oh, yes. I'll get it for you right away," he said. He scurried from the office, returned in a few minutes, and handed me an envelope. "You may be sure that this is creating quite a little impression in the company here," he said.

I opened the envelope and looked at the contents. It held thirty one-hundred-dollar bills. "It would stir up a few things in the New York office, too," I observed. "Parting with this much money doesn't mean any more to Martin Raymond than making five donations a day to the blood bank. Well, I'll see you around."

"I was thinking we might have lunch together," he said. He looked at his watch. "I belong to quite a good club. We could go a bit early."

"No, thanks," I said. "I hope to have half a day's work done by lunchtime. As you have already pointed out, I have only thirty days to try to do something that no one else has been able to do in almost seven years. Maybe I'll catch your club on the next trip to Cleveland."

"All right," he said, but he sounded disappointed. "How long do you think you'll be in Cleveland?"

"I have no way of knowing at the moment. Depends on what I dig up today, but I shouldn't be here long. After all, the case only starts here. There is one thing I'd like to ask you. It won't help the case, but I'm curious."

"What's that?"

"Were the policies on Rako sold through this office?"

"Yes."

"Why?"

"I'm afraid I don't understand," he said.

"Since Rako was a known criminal, why did you give him the insurance? Why wasn't he turned down on a morals clause?"

"There was no reason to," Hudson said, but he didn't sound too sure of himself. "His record was in the past. He had apparently reformed. He was an officer of a large union and also was active in a respectable trucking corporation."

"And the premiums on a million dollars of insurance come to a tidy sum," I said in disgust. "All right, Hudson, I'll try to pull your chestnuts out of the fire. But the next time, don't wait seven years before you scream for help."

I turned and left his office. Downstairs, in front of the building, I hailed a taxi and told the driver to take me to police headquarters. It was a short drive. I went inside and after a while got the attention of the desk sergeant.

"I am interested," I told him, "in a former Clevelander who disappeared several years ago. He had a record, and I would like to talk to someone who might know something about him. His name was, or is, Thomas Rako."

"Who are you?" the Sergeant asked.

"I work for an insurance company," I said.

He wasn't much impressed, but he picked up his phone and made a couple of calls. Finally he put the receiver down and looked at me. "Lieutenant Jameson will see you. Down that hall and the third door on the left."

I walked down a long corridor and found the third door. I knocked on it and a voice muttered something. I opened the door and went in. There was a man, gray-haired and beefy, sitting at a desk. He looked up as I entered.

"You the insurance dick?" he asked.

"That's right," I said.

"Got any identification?"

I took out my wallet and handed him several papers. He looked at them carefully, then glanced up as he returned them.

"Milo March, huh?" he said. "You're the guy who cracked

that case of the woman killing her husband. The dame we arrested yesterday."

"Yes."

"That was good work," he said grudgingly. "And now you're looking for Rako, huh? Starting a little late, aren't you?"

"A little," I admitted. "It was just handed to me on a silver platter this morning. About the only thing I can do is try."

"How come the insurance company is suddenly interested in him?"

"They just realized that in another month they may have to pay out a million dollars if Rako doesn't show up."

"That's a pretty good reason," he said. "I'm afraid that we can't help you much, March. Rako was never seen in Cleveland after he left for those Congressional hearings in Washington. We did a lot of checking on it, and the Federal men were here, too. A check was kept on his wife and all of his close friends, but nothing ever came of it."

"What do you think happened to him?"

"I think he was killed so he couldn't talk, but that's just between you and me. I can't prove it."

"Why wasn't his body ever found?"

He shrugged. "Maybe somebody put him in a bale of scrap metal and he ended up in a blast furnace. It's been known to happen."

"Yeah, I know."

"Sorry, March," he said, "but I don't think I can help you very much."

"I didn't expect you to tell me where he is," I said. "I just want to know a little about him. Our files contain the information that he had a record but there are not many details. What about that?"

The Lieutenant smiled. "Rako had a record, all right. It started when he was a kid. Petty theft, breaking and entering, car theft. He served time for all of those. Then he was arrested for assault and battery, assault with a deadly weapon, homicide three times. He beat all of those raps. The last time he was arrested was twelve years ago."

"How did he beat the raps?"

"Good lawyers and intimidation of witnesses—but I can't prove it."

"Then twelve years ago he reformed?" I asked. "That's what a character in the insurance company told me."

"Are you kidding? If Rako reformed, it was only when he couldn't breathe anymore. Rako got out of jail the last time twelve years ago. He went to work for Johnny Clark. Know who he is?"

"I know."

"He started out as a strong-arm boy for Clark. If anybody decided not to play along with Clark's union, it was Rako who paid him a visit. It was during that time that he was picked up on the assault and homicide charges. But he beat them. He became more and more important to Clark and moved up until he was head of the Carriers' local here, which is a catch-all local. That was when his wife went into business. You know about that?"

I nodded.

"That was what led to Rako being called before the committee," he continued.

"It was believed that Rako's wife and Clark's wife were given union funds to start the business, and that various companies here were blackmailed into throwing their business to the Rack Trucking Company. That's what the Congressional committee was trying to find out about. But they were never able to prove anything and neither was anyone else. You know about Rako taking the Fifth?"

"Yes. He took it on every question for a whole day and then disappeared that night."

"That's right. And I can tell you that the trail ended right there—at the Peraton Hotel in Washington where Rako was staying. A lot of good people have worked on it—the FBI, the investigators for the Congressional committee, and the police of several cities. Nobody ever got to where they could even see first base. And some of them have never stopped looking. That's what you're up against."

"I have a vague idea," I said dryly. "What kind of man was this Rako?"

"A smart hood."

"Really smart?"

"Smart enough. You figure it out. He started out like a hundred other punk kids. He got his education in the reform schools of the country. He got out of the can twelve years ago and went to work for Johnny Clark. Within three years he was beating every rap we tried to pin on him, and within another year he was partners with Johnny Clark in the trucking business—or their wives were. Clark has a lot of hoods working for him and most of them beat the raps against them, but not very many ever go into business with him."

"So why was Rako able to make it?"

He shrugged. "Your guess is as good as mine."

"I have a guess," I said. "I'm not a specialist on Johnny Clark, but I do know he has a lot of hoods working for him and some of them are big time. As you say, Clark doesn't go into partnership with all of them. So my guess would be that in that first four years that Rako worked for Clark, he got something on him."

He looked at me shrewdly. "Just between us, that was my guess years ago. But how do you prove a thing like that?"

"Usually, you don't. I'm not trying to now. But let's assume that it's a good guess and then carry it a step farther. Rako is up before a Congressional committee and takes the Fifth about a hundred times. He's bound to be cited for contempt and draw at least a year in jail. Plus the fact that they'll keep after him. He doesn't want to spend a year in the Big House and Clark doesn't want him to talk. Clark could handle this easily, except for the fact that Rako has other things on him. And since Rako is smart, whatever he has is in a safe place and will be turned over to the authorities if anything happens to him. So he goes to Clark and makes a deal. If Clark will help him to disappear and furnish him enough money, they'll both be safe. How does that sound?"

"It could make sense," Jameson said, "but can you prove it in thirty days?"

"I don't know, but I'm going to give it a hell of a try."

"A lot of men have been giving it a hell of a try for more than six years."

"I know, but I have one advantage. They were official and I'm not. I can do things that they couldn't."

"You mean stuff like wiretaps?"

"Hell, no," I said. "You and I both know that they use wire-taps and bugs all the time. I have a system of my own, but it wouldn't work if I had to account to the public."

"Mind if I ask what it is?"

"No. I just stick around the central characters and I keep pushing until they get off balance. When that happens, some-body talks or they get too eager to push back, and then they make mistakes. It's simple enough."

"And dangerous," he said. "But it might work. It might also get you in trouble with the local cops."

"I've been in trouble with cops, too," I said, "but you tell me a better way."

"If I had one, I would have solved the case myself. Is that the way you wrapped up the other case here?"

I nodded. "I pushed until the doctor decided to kill me. He made his mistake then, and when his plan didn't work, he and the widow both fell apart like wet paper cartons."

"Well, I wish you luck," he said. "Sorry I can't help more."

"There are a couple of things I'd still like to ask you," I said. "What about Mrs. Rako? She still in town?"

"She lives up in Cleveland Heights." He opened a drawer and rummaged through it until he found what he wanted. He copied something down on a piece of paper and shoved it across to me. "There's her address. I don't think you'll get much out of her. She's been pretty well worked over the last few years."

"Is the trucking company still in business?"

"Sure. The Rack Trucking Company. It does a lot of busi-ness here and throughout Ohio."

"Still the same owners?"

"Yes—Mrs. Rako and Mrs. Clark."

"How come?"

"They both swore it was their own money that went into the company, and nobody could prove differently. They also claim that they get no extra business because Johnny Clark is the head of the Carrier Workers Union, and nobody could prove that they did. So they're still in business."

"Nice," I said. "You got any mug shots of Rako?"

"Sure. Lots of them, but they're twelve years old."

"Can I take a look at them?"

He nodded and reached for the phone. He told someone I'd be down to look at the pictures of Thomas Rako and hung up. "Go back to the entrance, take the corridor to your right, and it's the second door on the right."

"Thanks," I said, and meant it, "for everything."

"You're welcome," he said. He looked up, giving me a twisted smile. "Good luck. You'll need it."

"I know," I told him, and left. I followed his directions and ended up with a police technician. He had the mug shots ready for me. They showed a heavyset, black-haired man who looked like a hundred other young thugs.

"They're pretty old," the technician said. "Why don't you try one of the newspapers? They'll probably have pictures taken just before he disappeared."

"That's a good suggestion. Thanks. I'll try them."

He looked at me curiously. "It's a long time since he went into the wild blue yonder. You going to try to find him?"

"That's the general idea," I said. "And I can't say I'm too

crazy about it. But you know how it is, a dollar here and a dollar there."

"Private dick?"

"Just as bad. Insurance dick."

He smiled. "Well, if you find him, tell him he ought to come in and pose for a new picture."

"I'll do that."

I left police headquarters and went over to the *Cleveland Plain Dealer*. I talked to a couple of people and finally I was handed a folder with Rako's name on it. It was full of clippings. I thumbed through them until I found one that had a picture of Rako at the time he left the hearing room of the committee. It was obviously the same man I'd seen in the mug shots, but he'd changed. Not just that he was a little older; he'd taken on some polish. His clothes were better and he wore them as though he knew it. He'd taken on a little weight, too, probably from eating better. I thanked the man who'd given me the folder and left.

It was already noon. I stepped in at one of the hotels and had a couple of martinis and some lunch. Then I found a taxi and told the driver to take me to the address in Cleveland Heights.

When we arrived, I saw a fairly modern house that must have cost about thirty thousand. It was in a good neighborhood. There was a Dodge, maybe a year old, in the driveway. It didn't look like the sort of place where it would be easy to get a taxi, so I told the driver to wait. I walked up to the house and rang the bell.

The door was opened by a very attractive woman, short, with black hair, about thirty-five years old. "Yes?" she said.

"I'm looking for Mrs. Rako," I said.

"I'm Mrs. Rako. What is it?"

"My name is Milo March. I represent the company that sold your husband his insurance policies. I'd like to talk to you for a few minutes."

She turned and went back into the house, leaving the door open so I could follow. She led the way into the living room. It was nicely, and expensively, furnished, but at the moment it was in a state of disorder. There were several empty glasses on the coffee table and the ashtrays were full.

"It's the maid's day off and I haven't had a chance to clean up," she said. It was an explanation, not an apology. "Can I give you a cup of coffee?"

"No, thanks."

"A drink, then?"

"That I'll take," I said.

She disappeared into the next room. I sat down and lit a cigarette. She was soon back with a drink—one drink—which she handed to me.

"Aren't you joining me?" I asked.

She shook her head. "It's a little too early for me."

"You're younger than I thought you would be," I observed.

She smiled. "It's nice of you to say that, but I'm not as young as I'd like to think I am. And Tom would be forty—if he were still alive."

"You're sure he's dead?" I asked.

"Aren't you?" she replied, her eyes widening.

"I don't know," I admitted. "You must not have been married long when he disappeared."

"A little more than three years."

I looked around the room again. "You seem to have managed pretty well."

"Oh, we already owned this home. And I had my own savings account. Then I had my own business, and it's been doing quite well. Now my lawyer tells me that I'll be getting the insurance money in about a month."

"That's a possibility. What do you think you'll do then, Mrs. Rako?"

"Just go on as I have been. This is my home and I like it, and I also like my business."

"You're not thinking of moving—say, abroad?"

"No. Why should I?"

"Some people might think that when your husband vanished he left the country and went somewhere, perhaps Europe or South America, to live, and that after you collect the insurance you might join him."

"What a horrible thing to think," she said. She blinked her eyes as though to avoid crying, but I didn't see any tears.

"Maybe so. But the insurance money will add up to a pretty decent income for seven years."

"Well, I intend to stay right here, Mr. March."

"All right, Mrs. Rako. How did you happen to go into business with Mrs. Clark?"

"Well, we both had some money of our own and we were tired of doing nothing, so we decided to go into business."

"How did you decide on trucking?"

"Our lawyers told us it was a good investment."

"It had nothing to do with the fact that your husbands were important in the Carrier Workers Union?"

"Of course not. This was something we were determined to do on our own."

"I see," I said. "Well, it makes an interesting story." She leaned forward in her chair. "All the things you're asking, Mr. March, have been asked a thousand times by the police, the FBI, and a dozen Congressional investigators. If there had been anything wrong with our business, don't you think they would have discovered it?"

"Maybe. Tell me, Mrs. Rako, did you know your husband had a police record when you married him?"

"Of course. But that was all in the past. He had a good job with Mr. Clark and he never did anything wrong again."

"What did he do for Mr. Clark?"

"Well, at first he was an organizer. You know, he was sent to anyplace where the union was having trouble and he straightened things out."

"I'll bet."

"Then later he was sent here to be the business manager of Local 97. That's a very important local."

"Mrs. Rako," I said abruptly, "what do you think happened to your husband?"

"I don't know," she said. "Maybe he was the victim of a hit-and-run driver and the body couldn't be identified. Or maybe he was held up and killed for his money."

"Was he carrying much?"

"He always carried between two and three thousand dollars."

"That's a nice piece of change," I said. "But if that had happened, I think he would have been identified. I wasn't there, but I'm sure that the police were thorough enough to check the morgue and all the hospitals."

"He might have had amnesia and wandered off to some other city, where he was killed. They were very mean to him in that hearing and it might have given him amnesia."

"That's at least an unusual reason for amnesia. Did it ever occur to you that Johnny Clark might have killed him so he couldn't talk?"

"Oh, Mr. Clark wouldn't do anything like that. Besides there wasn't anything that Tom could have told that would hurt Mr. Clark in any way."

"Then why did he use the Fifth Amendment every time they asked him a question?"

"Because they were asking a lot of questions that were none of their business," she said indignantly.

"Did your husband have anything on Johnny Clark?" I asked. "Maybe something on paper and put away in a safe deposit box?"

"I never heard of such a thing!" she exclaimed. "What a terrible thing to say. Mr. Clark is a fine man, and my husband was no blackmailer. Why would he do a thing like that anyway?"

"It might ensure his getting help to vanish and being supplied with money wherever he is."

"Nonsense," she snapped. "Mr. March, I've tried very hard to cooperate with you, but I have had six years of policemen coming around and making insinuations about my husband and about me. It's my husband who's dead. I've lost something instead of gaining something as everybody seems to think. I'm getting tired of all these suggestions. If you're so sure my husband's alive, go out and find him."

"I intend to, honey," I said. I put the glass down and stood up. "Thanks for your help."

"You're welcome," she said, but she didn't mean it. She stood up and led the way back to the front door. She was angry and not so pretty now. She held the door open and I went through it and down to the waiting cab. I told the driver to take me back to where he'd picked me up.

When we got there I went into the nearest drugstore and looked up the Carrier Workers Union in the phone book. They had two numbers, Local 15 and Local 97. Both were at the same address, about two blocks from where I was. I walked over.

The whole building belonged to the union, but 97 had its own floor. I took the elevator up and stepped out into a swanky reception room. There was a sexy-looking blonde behind the desk.

"My name's March," I told her. "I'd like to see the business manager."

She nodded and picked up her phone. She gave my name, listened, then replaced the receiver. "You can go in," she said. "It's that door there."

I walked over and opened the door. Then I stopped. The man sitting behind the desk was Nick Potti, the owner of the club I'd been in the night before.

THREE

The surprise was all on my side, since he'd heard my name from the receptionist. He was sitting there smiling at me, but there was about as much warmth in it as you'd find on top of Mount Everest. His strong-arm boy was sitting in a chair in a corner of the office. He wasn't even bothering to smile.

"Well," I said, stepping into the office and closing the door, "I see you're a man of many interests. You run a club at night and a union in the day. It must be a profitable kind of moonlighting."

"I make out," he said. "I thought you were leaving Cleveland today, March."

"I was, but I got a new job that'll keep me here for a day or two."

"What's it got to do with me?"

"I didn't know it had anything to do with you until just now. I'm interested in a man named Thomas Rako."

"What're you trying to do, write a book on ancient history?"

"I'm trying to rewrite the future," I said. "Unless Rako shows up within thirty days, he will probably be declared legally dead."

"Ain't that a shame? Most people agreed that he was probably dead at least six years ago."

"Did you know him?"

"I knew him."

"What do you think happened to him?"

"I think those guys in Washington drove him so nuts that he flipped. Then maybe he walked into a car or maybe he went over to the river and took the big jump."

"Everybody has nice, neat little answers, don't they?" I said. "How come nobody ever guesses that maybe somebody put a bullet in him?"

"Why would anybody do that?"

"I wonder. Or maybe he didn't die at all. Maybe he's living somewhere under another name."

"That would be pretty dumb," Nick Potti said. "He had a good job and his nose was clean. Why would he walk out on that?"

"I can think of a lot of reasons, all of them named Johnny Clark. Tell me something, Nick. Was Rako a valuable employee of the union?"

"Sure he was."

"Did the union do anything about looking for him?"

"Why should we? The cops were looking for him and they got more experience at it than we have."

"You know the Rack Trucking Company here in Cleveland?"

"Sure. They got a union contract with us."

"I don't suppose they get any extra jobs because they're owned by Johnny Clark's wife and Rako's wife?"

"Of course not. Why should they?"

"I like your innocence, Nick," I said. "Do you think that Rako had something on Johnny Clark?"

"What do you mean?"

"It's simple—even simple enough for you, Nick. You'd have to be pretty dumb not to see that Rako knew things that could have hurt Johnny Clark and the Carrier Workers. Otherwise he wouldn't have taken the Fifth Amendment so often. That put him in line for a possible year behind bars for contempt. And the pressure would have stayed on him. This brings up two interesting possibilities. Somebody might have decided that a dead partner is better than a loyal one, or Rako might have had enough information somewhere to demand that he be gotten out of it."

The strong-arm man stirred in his chair. "Boss," he said pleadingly.

"Shut up, Rocks," Nick Potti said without taking his gaze off me. "Look, March, we don't like snoopers around here, no matter what kind they are. We especially don't like them when they make cracks like that. Even the Feds have been trying to pin stuff on us for years and didn't get nowhere, so that means we're clean, see? The quicker you wise up to that, the better off you'll be. I don't know what your angle is, but it ain't going to get you no farther than the corner bar. Are you planning on being in Cleveland long?"

"Not very long," I said cheerfully. "I'm going to go to Washington. I understand Johnny Clark has his office there."

"I don't care where you go. Just get lost. And stay that way."

"Oh, I'll probably see you tonight. Or you'll see me through that one-way glass of yours."

"You're not welcome at my club," he said tightly.

"I wasn't expecting any red carpet. But you're running a public place and you can't keep me out as long as I behave and pay my way. And keep your pet goon out of my way. The next time I might hurt him." I walked to the door and opened it. "I'll make you a bet, Nick. Ten to two that you're on the phone to Johnny Clark as soon as I get out of here."

"Go to hell," he said hoarsely.

I smiled at him and left, closing the door gently. Then I went directly back to my hotel. When I got there I phoned police headquarters and asked for Lieutenant Jameson. "This is Milo March," I said when he came on.

"Found Rako already?" he asked.

"Not quite, but people are learning that I'm around. I've been ordered out of a house and out of the city."

"Who ordered you out of the city?"

"Nick Potti."

He grunted. "So you tangled with him already?"

"Twice. Once last night at his club before I had this job and before I knew he had anything to do with the Carrier Workers, and again today at his other office. He's the one I'm calling about."

"What do you want to know?"

"I presume he has a record?"

"One going back more than twenty years. He's been charged with everything from homicide to simple assault. He started out as a strong-arm man and gun for one of the mobs here, then moved on to work for Johnny Clark. He hasn't been convicted often and then only for assault and carrying a gun. He's beaten all the big raps and he hasn't faced any more than questioning the past few years. He's a bigger man than Rako ever was—and more dangerous."

"Then how come he inherited Rako's job only after Rako vanished?"

"I don't know the answer to that one."

"What about the hood that Potti keeps around?"

"Rocks Mahoney? He's got a record as long as your arm—all of it for rough stuff. He's not very bright, but Potti looks after him."

"All right. Thanks," I said.

"Watch out for Nick Potti, March," he said. "I can't prove it in court, but Potti is one of the three or four top professional killers in the country today."

"Thanks, I'll remember it. So long, Lieutenant."

"Good luck," he said and hung up.

Next I called the airlines and made a reservation on a flight to Washington leaving the next morning. After that I called room service and ordered a double drink. I took a fast shower while I was waiting for it. Then I shaved, had my drink, and stretched out on the bed.

It was a little after six when I awakened. I dressed slowly and went downstairs. The hotel bar was about half filled. I took one of the stools and ordered a dry martini. I sipped it slowly, watching and listening to the others in the bar. They were mostly couples, but there were a few men, obviously on business trips, sitting alone as I was. Nobody seemed to be very cheery, but then I don't suppose I looked cheery to them either. I had another martini and went into the dining room.

I stretched dinner out as long as I could, but it was still early when I left the hotel. I stopped in a bar on Euclid and had another drink and watched color television. The color didn't seem to help the stories any. Finally it was late enough and I walked on up the avenue to the club. It was just about time for Lola Crane to go on.

I headed for my usual table, but I was met by the headwaiter before I reached it.

"Sorry, sir," he said. "All the tables are reserved."

I looked over the room and saw that at least half of the tables were empty. "How do you know that I don't have a reservation?" I asked.

That stopped him but only for a couple of seconds. "I remember you, sir. You've been here for several nights. I'm sure I'd recall if you'd made a reservation. Would you like me to check the list to make certain?"

"Don't bother," I said. "I'm sure that you'd find that there was no room even if every table in the joint was empty. I'll sit at the bar."

"I'm not sure ... ," he began hesitatingly.

"I'm sure," I said pleasantly. "You can tell Nick Potti that if I don't get served, I'll immediately get a lawyer and start a suit against him on the grounds that my civil rights have been violated."

He scurried toward the back of the club. I glanced up at the glass mural on the back wall, knowing that Potti could see me, and waved. Then I went to the bar.

"I'll have a double V.O. on the rocks," I told the bartender.

He also looked uncertain. But he went off and started to make the drink. I noticed that he was moving very slowly. It took him as long to get ice in the glass as it should have to make several drinks. Finally he must have gotten some sort of signal, for he speeded up and came over with my drink.

"There you are, sir."

"Thank you," I said gravely as I paid him.

The small combo was already playing on the bandstand and about five minutes later Lola Crane came on. Her voice was just as spine-tingling as it had been the first night I heard her. I turned and beckoned the bartender.

"Would you get a message to Miss Crane for me?" I asked.

"I'm sorry, sir, it's against the regulations of the club."

I took a five-dollar bill from my pocket and held it so he could see it. "Would this help any?"

That really put a strain on him. He looked at the bill and licked his lips, then glanced at the glass mural. "I'm sorry—I can't," he said.

"All right. I'll take care of it myself. Bring me another drink." I left the five dollars on the bar and walked down to the bandstand. There was enough reflected light there so that she could see me, and she soon did. When she had recognized me, I indicated the bar with a motion of my head. She winked at me and I walked back to my stool.

When she'd finished her last number she came over and perched on the stool next to me. "Hello," she said. "Why aren't you at your usual table? I looked when I first came on."

"I was told earlier by Nick Potti that I wasn't welcome in the club. I came anyway because it's my last night in Cleveland and I wanted to see you again. They said that all the tables were reserved, so I came to the bar."

The bartender was standing in front of us. "I'll have my

usual, Joe," she said. She waited until he went away. "Why?"

"I think it started last night because of you. Now it's a bit more complicated, but you're still a part of it. He acts as if he owned you."

"I think he acts that way about everybody who works for him," she said. "Ever since I came to work here he's been making passes—all uncompleted. I guess it didn't bother him too much at first, because I never mingled or went out with any of the customers or the boys in the band. He's the kind of man who thinks that all he has to do is wait and everything and everybody will fall into his hands. But then I went out with you last night. That must've started it."

"Want me to leave?" I asked.

She shook her head. "Not unless you want to. The worst he can do is fire me and have me blacklisted in a few other clubs around town. I can always get a job, even if it's in another city."

"There's no question about that, honey," I said. "I know a few places in New York City that would hire you in a minute. But as I said, the situation has become a little more complicated. It might not have anything to do with you, unless you know things about him that he wouldn't want you telling me."

"I don't know anything about him except what you hear from other singers and the musicians and the help. Even that I never paid much attention to. When you start working in nightclubs you soon learn that most club owners don't come out of Sunday schools." She looked up from her drink. "Milo, I didn't ask you anything about yourself last night. What … do you do for a living?"

"Not what you may be thinking right now," I said with a smile. "I'm an insurance investigator. And this has become more complicated because I'm looking for a former associate of Nick Potti's. I have a feeling that Nick and his friends don't want him found—alive or dead." I caught sight of a figure advancing between the tables. "We'd better change the subject for a minute. Here comes his pet goon. Tell me about the songs you're going to sing in the next show."

Without any sign of nervousness she switched to talking about her songs. I listened while I watched Rocks Mahoney get closer. As I'd guessed, he was heading for me.

"Hey, you," he said, stopping beside me. "Didn't you hear the boss say you ain't welcome here?"

"I heard him," I said evenly, "but I came anyway just to get some of the high-class booze you sell. You may be sure that I didn't come to see him—or you, for that matter. And I will feel no sense of loss if you leave quickly."

He scowled as if not sure whether he'd been insulted. "The boss wants to see you. Back in the office."

"Not tonight, chum. I'm busy."

He set himself more firmly on both feet. "The boss said I was to bring you back to the office."

I slipped off the stool and faced him. "And I said no. Don't try to take me. You've got too much glass in your jaw. If the boss wants to see me, he knows where I am. I might even buy him a drink if he comes down."

Rocks hesitated, not sure what to do.

"Run along, Rocks," I said softly. "You're only an errand boy, and this has already gotten too big for you to try any thinking about it. Just tell Nick that if he wants to see me I'm at the bar—because he instructed his headwaiter not to give me a table." I climbed back on my stool, but I kept watching him in the mirror.

"He ain't going to like it," Rocks muttered as he turned and trudged off.

I returned to the business at hand, which was a drink and Lola Crane. I noticed that the bartender was busy shining one small spot on the bar and was paler than the last time I had looked at him. I glanced at Lola. She was pale, too.

"Don't worry, honey," I told her. "It's all in a day's work. In singing you have to deal with creeps. In my business I have to deal with creeps, too. It's just that some days there are more of them around than other times."

"All right," she said. "But take care of yourself, Milo."

"I will, honey. Still want to see me after your last show?"

She nodded.

"Then run along. And if you know anybody who likes to bet, put a few dollars on the great man coming out of his office in a minute. I'll still be here when the last show is over."

She nodded again and left. The bartender was still polishing the bar. He moved over in front of me, rubbing industriously.

"Did you want another drink, sir?" he asked. His voice was so low I could barely hear it.

"Might as well. Let me finish this one now." I put the glass to my lips.

"You know what you're doing, mister?" he asked.

"I know, Joe."

"It's none of my business. It's just that I like Miss Crane. She's straight. And you're asking for trouble, a lot of trouble."

"I know. And thanks, Joe. I appreciate the interest—in Miss Crane. But I can take care of myself—and her, too, if necessary. It's going to be all right." I put the glass down on the bar, and he moved off with it. He brought it back, refilled, without another word.

It was five minutes before I had my next visitor. This time it was the headwaiter.

"Mr. March?" he asked politely, as if he'd never seen me before.

"Yes."

"Mr. Potti wishes to know if you'd join him at his table for a drink."

"Where's his table?" I asked.

"Over there, sir." He pointed to a table that was ringside but was still in the shadows. I could see that someone was sitting at it.

"I'll be happy to," I said. "Lead the way, my good man."

I finished my drink and followed him back through the tables. The orchestra was giving out with a nice jazz piece.

Nick Potti was sitting at the table alone. There were already two drinks on the table. His looked to be crème de menthe, but mine was a double V.O. There was a grim expression on Nick Potti's face; he looked like a violin string that had been drawn too tight.

"Hello, Nick," I said as I sat down. The headwaiter glided away. "It was nice of you to invite me for a drink."

"Cut it," he said. "What are you doing here, March?"

"You know what I'm doing here. I told you last night. You have a good singer and a good jazz combo. I came here because that's the kind of stuff I dig. There's no reason why I should stop coming just because I suddenly found out who you are. Besides, I don't think that's the reason you asked to see me."

"No?"

"No. I think you called Washington after I left today and were ordered to stay on top of me while I was in Cleveland and find out as much as you could." I smiled at him and raised my glass. "Shall we drink a toast to Thomas Rako?"

He made a sound deep in his throat but it wasn't a word. "I don't like you, March. I don't like you even a little bit. And people I don't like have a way of getting unhealthy. You might remember that."

"I'll remember it," I told him. "I started remembering it the minute I saw you in that other office today. But you might remember something, too. I don't care much for you either. And the people I don't like have a way of getting a long vacation—provided they manage to stay around long enough to get to that Big House. Do we understand each other?"

"Yeah," he said. He bit the word off as though it had a bad taste. "What're you doing in Cleveland, March? Rako hasn't been here in seven years."

"Where has he been, Nick?"

"How the hell do I know? Probably in a grave somewhere or wandering around not knowing who he is."

"Which would you put your money on, Nick?"

He said a short, ugly word. "You still didn't answer the question. What're you doing in Cleveland?"

"I was enjoying myself until you just butted in." I smiled at him. "I'll take you off the hook, Nick. You can tell Johnny Clark that I'll be in Washington sometime tomorrow and that I'll look him up after I get there." I finished my whiskey. "Thanks for the drink, Nick. I'd better get back to the bar before the headwaiter gets upset because I'm at one of the reserved tables."

"You can keep the table," he snapped. He stood up and looked down at me. "You'd better watch yourself, March."

"It's a habit I got into a long time ago and I can't seem to kick it. What's the matter, Nick? No harsh words about the fact that I was talking to your canary a few minutes ago?"

"I'm busy," he said.

He turned and walked away, his body held in check so he wouldn't be vulnerable.

I kept the table. The waiter came and served me, and when the last show was over Lola Crane joined me. She was nervous and continued to glance up at the glass mural.

We were on our second drink when she suddenly said, "Milo, let's get out of here."

"All right. Where do you want to go?"

She smiled. "The same bar we went to last night."

"An excellent idea. It was the best bar I've ever been in."

I paid the bill and we took a taxi to her apartment. One of the first things I did when I got there was put in a call to a club owner I knew in New York City. I introduced him to Lola on the phone and we played a tape of a couple of her songs. The call ended by her being offered a job.

It was the last time we talked business that night.

FOUR

I managed to get a few short hours of sleep at the hotel and then took a taxi to the airport. I slept on the plane most of the way to Washington. When I arrived, I took a taxi to the Peraton Hotel. It was a good hotel and it was also the place where Thomas Rako had been staying at the time he disappeared.

I checked into the hotel and was taken up to my room. The bellboy checked everything and then waited to be rewarded. I gave him five dollars. His eyes widened as he saw the number on the bill. He looked up at me and waited. He knew that big a tip demanded extra service.

"How long have you worked here?" I asked.

"Two years, sir."

"Is there anybody on the staff who was here seven years ago?"

"Yes, sir. The bell captain was and there is one bellhop who's been here that long. And I believe the night clerk and several of the room-service waiters have, too. I wouldn't know about other staff members."

"What's your name?"

"Freddie."

"Okay, Freddie, thanks for everything. If I need something I'll ask for you."

"Yes, sir," he said, and took off.

When he was gone, I phoned down to room service and asked them to send up a bottle of V.O. and some ice. I took off my jacket and shirt and went in and shaved while I was waiting. The liquor arrived just as I came out of the bathroom. I let the waiter in and signed the check. I made myself a good stiff drink, lit a cigarette, and relaxed.

When I'd finished the drink, I went in and took a hot shower. Then I unpacked and got dressed. I put the suit I'd been wearing on the bed, called valet service, and asked them to pick it up for pressing and have it back in the morning.

I was still tired, but feeling better than I had when I'd arrived. I had one more drink and left the hotel. I got a taxi in front and told the driver to take me to the Carrier Workers building.

It was quite a place, all steel and glass, about ten stories high. I wondered how much in dues it had taken to build it. I went inside. There was a huge lobby on the ground floor, furnished in modernistic style, with a large curved reception desk. The blonde behind the desk was modernistic, too.

I looked around as I walked over to the desk. There were two men sitting in chairs to the left. They both glanced at me casually, then went back to reading their magazines. I switched my gaze back to the blonde. She looked even better at close range.

"Where will I find Mr. Clark?" I asked.

"Do you have an appointment?" she countered.

"No, but I think he'll see me."

"Just a minute," she murmured. She picked up one of the phones on her desk and pushed a button on it. "There's a gentleman down here who would like to see Mr. Clark." She waited a minute. "All right." She replaced the phone.

She glanced briefly across the lobby and it seemed to me that she nodded ever so slightly, then her gaze came back to me. "Take the elevator to the penthouse. Mr. Clark's secretary will talk to you."

"Thank you," I said. I walked to the elevators and stepped into one. I was aware that someone followed me in, but I didn't look around immediately. The elevator was self-operated. I pushed the button marked P and the doors closed silently. I shifted my position so I could see my fellow passenger.

He hadn't bothered to push a button. Obviously he was going to the same floor as I was. He was leaning against the wall of the elevator, studying his manicured fingernails and ignoring me. I decided I'd been right about the nod. He was one of the two men who had been sitting in the lobby when I entered. He was tall and thin, with hair the color of straw and a pale, bloodless face. His suit was expensive and well tailored, but not so well as to completely conceal a slight bulge under his left arm.

The elevator stopped and I stepped out into a more luxurious reception room than the ground floor one. There was another elegant receptionist, this one with dark hair. She looked up and waited for me to approach. I was aware that the other man had followed me from the elevator, but he was staying behind me.

"You're the gentleman who wants to see Mr. Clark," she said before I could open my mouth. She didn't even wait for me to nod. "I'm Mr. Clark's secretary. Do you have an appointment?"

"No. I think, however, he'll see me if you tell him my name. I'm Milo March."

Although nothing changed in her expression, I had the feeling that she knew my name. She reached for the intercom on her desk and said, "A Mr. Milo March is here to see you, Mr. Clark."

"Send him right in," a voice said heartily.

She glanced up. "You may go in, Mr. March. Straight back at the end of the corridor."

I walked back, heading for what looked like a solid mahogany door. I sensed rather than heard the other man following me. When I got there, I opened the door and stepped inside.

It was quite an office, running the whole width of the building. Outside there was a terrace almost as large. Through the glass wall you could see a large part of Washington. Everything was on a big scale, but the biggest thing in the room was the desk. The man behind it was tall and muscular. Most women would probably have called him handsome. His clothes were expensive and in good taste. He looked like a successful businessman—which I suppose he was.

"So you're Johnny Clark," I said.

"I'm Johnny Clark," he answered. He sounded satisfied with the fact. "Come in and sit down."

"What about my constant companion?" I asked, pointing a thumb over my shoulder. "Is he joining us, or did he just come along to see that I didn't get lost?"

Clark laughed. It was a big, hearty laugh, but there was no

feeling in it. It was something he'd learned to do just as he'd learned to wear the right clothes.

"Come on in and sit down, Jerry," he said.

The door closed behind me and the blond man moved into sight. He went over to a chair and sat down.

"This is Jerry Dell," Clark said. "He's one of my secretaries."

"I noticed he carries his typewriter in a shoulder holster," I observed.

Clark laughed again. "I have to have protection. A lot of guys would like to get rid of Johnny Clark. They've been trying for a long time." He pointed to a chair beside his desk. "Sit down, Milo. Cigarette? Cigar?"

I took the chair and pulled out my own cigarettes. "No, thanks."

"Drink?"

"I might try that."

"Jerry," he said without looking around, "bring us two drinks. I'll have bourbon, a little water. Milo?"

"V.O. or Canadian Club on the rocks."

He nodded and Jerry Dell got up and went to the bar. It was at the far end of the room next to a wall that seemed to include a TV set, a fancy radio, a phonograph console, and what I thought was a tape-recording outfit—all built in.

"Quite a place you have here, Mr. Clark," I said.

"Call me Johnny. Everybody does. Yeah, it's a nice building. Not only that, it's bug-proof. They can't even use those fancy gadgets that'll pick up sound right through a wall. We've got them screened out. And we got plenty of devices in here that'll pick up any kind of a bug they try to plant inside. Of course, they can still tap our telephones, but only with the help of the phone company, because we have our own terminal box right here in the building. But that's all right. Might as well let them have a little fun." He smiled and you could see that he was very pleased with himself.

"Sounds like quite a building," I said. "Incidentally, who are 'they'?"

"The Justice Department, Hoffa's boys, some of the big companies, or any stray cops that get an itch to be big men."

Jerry Dell brought the drinks over and retreated to his chair.

"Tell me, Milo," Clark said, "why were you so sure that I'd see you just because of your name?"

I took a drink. "That one's easy. I offered to bet Nick Potti ten to two that he'd be on the phone to you within five minutes after I left his union office. He wouldn't bet. Then it was easy to guess that he'd call you again last night as soon as he found out I was coming to Washington this morning. From that it was even easier to figure that you'd be expecting me."

He laughed again. "Smart. I like smart guys. Why are you looking for Tom Rako?"

"A million dollars in insurance. Half to Mrs. Rako and half to the company owned by your wife and Mrs. Rako. In another thirty days the courts could declare Rako legally dead and the insurance would have to be paid. I doubt if there's any question that the courts will be petitioned to do just that."

He looked at me curiously. "You think you can find him?"

"I can try."

"You know that every FBI man and most of the cops in the country have been trying for almost seven years?"

"I know." I nibbled on my drink and waited.

"Why do you come to us?"

"Why not? He was one of your boys, and I've always heard that you look after your own. I thought maybe you'd like to have Rako found."

"We offered a reward at the time. It's still good."

"I wasn't looking for a reward. I thought I might get some information."

"What kind?"

"What do you think happened to Thomas Rako?"

He shrugged. "Maybe he got mugged for his roll and died, or had amnesia and wandered off. Or maybe he didn't like the threats the committee was making and took a powder."

"I don't care much for the mugging theory," I said. "It sounds too much like cheap melodrama. Suppose he took a powder. To get away with it and to continue to get away with it this long, he'd need help. And who would a man turn to but his friends?"

"Meaning us?"

"That was the general idea."

"Lots of people have thought of that, friend," he said. "There's nothing to it. Ask the Feds. They've looked into everything they could without being able to prove a thing."

"I wasn't trying to prove anything. I was asking."

"Well, we didn't help him," he said shortly. He was showing signs of getting restless.

It was time to get him interested again. I put my glass down on the desk and lit a cigarette. "There are a couple of other possible theories about Rako," I said gently. "According to the Congressional committee, Rako was a very important witness against you. They seemed to feel that if they could get him to talk, they'd have a case. He took the Fifth Amendment that day seven years ago, but they might have been able to break him down. Only if he were alive, though. That thought might have occurred to you and you might have taken care to prevent it."

For a brief minute the steel of Johnny Clark showed through his expression; then his face relaxed and he laughed. "That's not very original either. A lot of cops thought about it. The result was the same. Nothing. Anyway, Tom Rako had nothing to tell."

"Then why did he take the Fifth?"

"He resented the invasion of his privacy."

"I'm glad to see that you have a sense of humor," I said gravely. "There is another possibility, Johnny. As I said, Rako was an important witness. By refusing to answer, he put himself in line for a contempt charge and a year in jail. He also knew they'd never let up on him. So he went to his good friend and benefactor, Johnny Clark, and said he wanted to disappear. All he needed was a little help and a little money. It wasn't so much to ask, and maybe he got it."

"Why would I do a thing like that?"

"I have a theory about that, too," I said easily. "Rako came up in your organization fast, passing men with even bigger reputations. He made a lot of money and his wife went into business with your wife. Why? Maybe he had something on you. Maybe he still had it at the time of the hearings, and maybe it was put away in some safe place so that if anything happened to him it would end up in the hands of the Justice Department. I think that if he asked for help under those circumstances, he'd get it."

There was a moment of silence. Jerry Dell was sitting motionless, staring at me, but he gave the impression of a well-trained watchdog waiting for orders to pounce.

"You talk like a big man," Johnny Clark said, his voice hard. "So you're just a cop trying to nail Johnny Clark. There's nothing new about that. You're only another punk. Maybe one that makes a little more dough than the other cops, but still a punk. And I know how to handle punks."

"That's more or less what I was suggesting," I said.

"I'm clean," he said. "Nobody can pin anything on me. I run a twenty-million-dollar-a-year business. The business makes money and everybody in it makes money. Ask any of the guys in my union. They're getting more money and more benefits than they ever got in their lives before. They'll tell you."

"I've also heard that the ones who feel otherwise either are no longer around or have learned the hard way to keep their mouths shut."

"Talk's cheap. Could you run a twenty-million-dollar business? Could any of those other cops? So everybody thinks he'll get on Johnny Clark's back and then he'll be a big man. It doesn't work that way, friend. You climb on Johnny Clark's back and you're liable to get a lump on the head from crashing into a solid brick wall."

"Or from one of your secretaries?" I suggested.

The anger went out of him as suddenly as it had come. He leaned back and laughed. "You're smart, Milo. I like smart guys. You thought you'd get under my skin and maybe you'd learn something. Well, it doesn't work that way. I'm clean. Nobody can touch me. You go right out and find Tom Rako. You can even collect a reward from us—for information leading to the whereabouts of Thomas Rako, dead or alive. Five grand."

"You mean it's all right if I shoot him when I find him?"

"I didn't say that. It's worded that way so if anybody even finds his grave somewhere, they can still collect. Now, you don't have much time to find Tom. You'd better get started."

I stood up and looked down at him. "Thanks for the talk."

"Always glad to talk to cops," he said. He gave me that arrogant smile again. "It's the only way I get laughs. Did you get what you came after?"

"I may have." I walked to the door and turned to look at him. I noticed that Jerry Dell was already standing up, ready to follow me. "I'll let you in on something, Clark. You may or may not have had anything to do with the disappearance of Thomas Rako. I don't even care. But somebody did have something to do with it, and somebody had something to gain by it. I'm just getting the information around that whoever it was is in for trouble in the near future."

"What does that mean? What kind of trouble?"

"My kind," I said. For the first time I smiled at him. "I don't like you, Clark. I don't like anything about you, but I understand how you got where you are. You're a pusher. So am I. When I'm after something I push anybody who's even near the scene. And I do all of my own pushing—without the help of secretaries. That's my kind of trouble. If you're as clean as you say you are, then you have nothing to worry about. If you're not, you'd better tell your boys to put their galoshes on. The last thirty days are going to be the toughest."

His anger was back. His face worked, trying to produce the usual laugh, but it didn't quite come off. "Get out," he said.

I turned and marched down the corridor. I knew that Jerry Dell was following me, but I didn't bother to look back. I marched past the dark-haired secretary and into the elevator, which was still waiting. The blond gunman stepped in after me and I punched the button. We rode down in complete silence.

When the door opened, I walked through the lobby, past the receptionist, to the front. I was just about to step outside when Dell spoke for the first time.

"March," he said. His voice was soft, almost effeminate.

I turned to look at him. "I didn't know you talked," I said. "I thought you only took dictation."

He was staring at me and there was a strange expression— excitement—in his eyes. "The chief is a nice, polite guy and he puts up with all you crumbs. But I got a message for you. Lay off. If you don't, I'm going to see you, baby."

"Don't bother, baby," I said. "Stay home and nurse your wrist—before it becomes too limp to use a gun."

I turned and went through the doors.

FIVE

I walked a block before I looked back. He hadn't followed me from the building. I knew I'd stirred him up, as I'd meant to. If I was right in my suspicions about Clark, Jerry Dell would be begging for the assignment, and his very eagerness would be a slight advantage for me. I went down the street until I came to a drugstore. I wanted to see Robert Salem, who had been the committee's counsel seven years before. I had read somewhere that he was now working for one of the government departments. The question was which one.

There was one newspaperman in Washington I knew slightly. He was George Macklin, a political columnist on the *Washington Ledger.* I called the paper and asked for him. He came on a moment later.

"This is Milo March," I said. "I met you about a year ago in New York City at the press club."

He was silent for a moment. "March?" he said. "You're the insurance investigator, aren't you? A friend of Williams of the *Bulletin?* Right?"

"Right. I hope you don't mind me calling you."

"Not at all." His voice sounded warmer. "I remember now. You and Williams and I tied one on and pub-crawled all over town. Are you in Washington?"

"Yes. Just for a day or two."

"Then maybe I can repay the favor and show you some of our better pubs."

"That might be fun," I said. "In the meantime, I was wondering if you could give me some information."

"What kind?"

"I'm trying to locate Robert Salem. He used to be the counsel for the House committee on labor unions—about seven years ago."

"I remember," he said. His voice was sharper, as though he sensed there might be something for him in it. "He works in Commerce now. Chief counsel. Do you know him?"

"No, but I want to see him."

"A story in it?"

"There might be, but you'd have to sit on it for a while."

"How about meeting me for drinks tonight?"

"I'm not sure about tonight. I think tomorrow would be better."

"How about lunch at twelve-thirty?"

"Fine."

"Meet me at the press—no, that's no good. It'll be full of thieving reporters who'll be sure that I'm on a story if I'm not playing gin rummy. Meet me at the Lido. It's a little restaurant about four blocks south of the club."

"I'll be there."

"Fine. We'll have lunch and plan our evening. Glad you called." He hung up.

I looked up the number of the Department of Commerce and called it. I asked for Robert Salem but got his secretary.

"I'd like to speak to Mr. Salem," I said.

"Who's calling, please?"

"My name is March, but I'm afraid it won't mean anything to him. Tell him I want to talk to him about the work he was doing seven years ago."

"Just a minute, please."

The line went dead and I waited. About two minutes went by and then Salem himself came on.

"This is Robert Salem. Who did you say you were?"

"My name is Milo March. I represent the Intercontinental Insurance Company. I'd like to talk to you for a few minutes."

"What about?"

"Thomas Rako."

There was a few seconds of silence. "All right," he said crisply. "Be here in thirty minutes." There was a click as the connection was severed.

I went out and hailed a taxi. I told the driver to take me to the Department of Commerce and settled back in the seat. We had driven five or six blocks when quite by accident I discovered that there was a car following my cab. I checked three or four more times, and there was no doubt about it. I smiled to myself. I was sure that Jerry Dell didn't go off working on his own; it meant that Johnny Clark was more concerned than he'd pretended to be.

We reached the Commerce Building and after a few false starts I found Salem's office. I had to wait about ten minutes and then I was shown into his room. I was greeted by a thin, tense-looking young man, younger than I was. I'd forgotten how very young he'd been when he was with the committee. He gave me a brisk handshake and motioned me to a chair.

"What's your interest in Rako?" he asked.

"I'm interested in finding him."

He smiled thinly. "A little late, isn't it?"

"Not too late to be interested," I said. "I got the case yesterday from the insurance company. In thirty days Rako can be declared legally dead and they have to shell out one million dollars. So they suddenly pushed the panic button."

"Why'd they wait so long?"

"I guess they were hoping the FBI would pull their chestnuts out of the fire for them."

He smiled again. "You think you can accomplish in a month what the FBI couldn't do in almost seven years?"

"Maybe. I work a little differently and sometimes it pays off. Do you remember the case?"

"I remember it. I lived it for four years, Mr. March—one year before he disappeared to three years afterwards. What do you want to know?"

"As much as we can cram into the time you're giving me. First, what do you think happened to Rako?"

"Off the record, I think one of two things. Either Johnny Clark had him killed or Johnny Clark helped him to get away. I can't prove it, neither can the Justice Department."

"Any idea where he headed for?"

Salem shook his head. "The trail started and ended at the Peraton Hotel. That day when the committee recessed, Rako went from the hearing room to the Carrier Workers' headquarters. He was there about an hour, then left. An hour after that he showed up at the hotel carrying some packages which apparently contained clothing, and went to his room. A little later he ordered a drink and dinner from room service. So far as we can find out, nothing more has been heard of Rako since then. When he didn't show up the next morning, he was sent for. The dinner and drink were still in his room, untouched. All of Rako's clothes were still there. But he wasn't."

"Nobody saw him leave the hotel?"

"Nobody saw him leave. He had no phone calls. Nobody noticed him have any visitors. But he may have had one."

"Why do you say that?"

"Somebody wiped the doorknob clean of any prints. There was no reason for Rako to do that. His prints were on record, and there were plenty of his prints on things inside the room."

"How come it wasn't discovered until the next morning? Room service should have gone up to get the dinner dishes out."

"Rako told them not to bother him, that he was going to bed right after he ate."

"What about Clark and his various punks?"

"All of them had perfect alibis. We checked out all the ones that were in Washington—or that we knew were in Washington."

"Some of his men could have come in from another city."

"They could have, but there was never any proof, and there were plenty of attempts to get it."

"Rako was an important witness, wasn't he?"

"The most important. At least, in terms of what I think he could have told."

"Why? Was the trucking company owned by Mrs. Rako and Mrs. Clark that important?"

"Actually," he said slowly, "that was one of the minor items. It was my belief then, as it is now, that Rako knew more about Clark's operations than anybody else. If you go back and read the record, you'll see that we questioned him about where a lot of money went, about three killings, any number of assault and intimidation cases, and payoffs to Clark from various trucking companies."

"He took the Fifth on all of them?"

"On everything except his name and address. And we weren't through with him."

"Why? He wasn't going to answer, and you had enough for a contempt charge."

He nodded. "But we wanted to let him know that the pressure was on him and that it was going to stay there. We had a lot more information on his activities—we couldn't prove any of it, but I was sure it was accurate—and we felt that sooner or later Rako would break under the pressure and make a deal. If not then, when he went to prison. You see, we knew one thing about him that even Clark didn't know."

"What was that?"

"The last time he was in prison, he was an informant. Nobody knew this except the warden."

"That is interesting." I said. "Back to your two theories. I had already arrived at the same conclusions. There is something else that occurred to me, but I may be way out in left field. I haven't had much time on it."

"What is it?"

"Rako seems to have come up in Clark's outfit pretty fast. On the way he passed men with bigger records as tough boys and better for the organization. According to the Cleveland police, Rako was never much more than a strong-arm punk until after he went to work for Clark. Then suddenly he's in the money and doing important jobs, even to heading Clark's catch-all union local in Cleveland. Why?"

"What's your guess?"

"That early after he started working for Clark, he got something on him. If so, it must've been big and he must've found some way of convincing Clark that if anything happened to him, it would end up with the police. If that's all true, when he wanted to run he could make Clark help him get away and furnish him money. How does that sound? Too wild?"

He put the tips of his fingers together and stared out the window. "I think," he said carefully, "that was very astute of you, Mr. March. I long entertained the same thought. In fact, I can offer you one piece of information in support of it. Note, however, that I said information, not proof, although I think that it's pretty strong circumstantial evidence."

"What's that?"

"The day that Rako was last seen, a check for seventy-five thousand dollars was cashed by the Carrier Workers' national office here. The cashing of the check was okayed personally by Johnny Clark. There is no record anywhere to indicate the destination of that money. There was a break in the hearings that day for lunch. Rako had lunch with Johnny Clark. We reconvened the hearings at one-thirty. The check was cashed at approximately two o'clock. When the hearing recessed for the day, Rako went directly to the Carrier Workers' office."

"When did you learn this?"

"About a year later. We continued to investigate Clark and the Carrier Workers for another three years after Rako's disappearance. The only thing we found on the seventy-five thousand was the check stub and the canceled check. The stub carried Clark's initials, showing that he had approved it. But we were never able to find any records showing where the money went. Those records, if there were ever any, have vanished."

"Clark was questioned?"

"Oh, yes, for two days. If you ever care to look up the records, you will find that Johnny Clark is a very interesting man. He was always affable; he cooperated in every way; he never took the Fifth, but answered every question fully and eagerly. In fact, he answered every question in such detail that when you examine the answer you discover he had said nothing. In this particular case several hundred pages of testimony boiled down to the fact that he thought the money had gone to one of the locals to help it out. But he wasn't sure of that and he couldn't remember which local it was— if it had gone to one. He had no idea what had happened to the records. He thought the money had been repaid, but he wasn't sure of that either. But obviously it had been spent for legitimate union business or he wouldn't have approved of it. And on and on and on."

"Was it investigated further?"

"Yes. We checked constantly with Justice, and when the committee was finally dissolved, we turned our complete files over to that department. But the only thing known about the check is what Johnny Clark told us. He was very sorry about the state of records, but he did have a big job and what could he do about it?"

"Can you run a twenty-million-dollar business?" I said in a fair imitation of Clark's voice. "Can any of those cops?"

He smiled. "I see you've met Johnny Clark."

"I just came from there."

He looked surprised. "Looking for clues?"

"No. I told you I work differently. Do you think I can get any information from the Justice Department?"

"I don't think so. They are not supposed to give out information except to actual police officials. However, I don't think they could add a lot to what I've told you that would help. Only detail. Which is also all you'd really get from going over the published records of the hearings. The only thing they could give you would be information that would keep you from duplicating useless work that has already been done. But I don't think they'll give you anything."

"That's the way I figured it," I said. "Anything else you can tell me?"

"Nothing that I can think of at the moment."

"Any other large cash withdrawals by the union in the last seven years?"

"Oh, many. Perhaps some went to Rako, but there were more big withdrawals than Clark would give Rako, no matter what he had on Clark. Again no records. And the books always balance perfectly."

"If Rako took the seventy-five thousand and ran, where do you think he'd go?"

He was thoughtful for a minute. "My guess was, and is,

Brazil. There's been a lot of checking down there, but it doesn't mean he isn't in the country."

"What's Rako's ancestry?"

"I don't know precisely. Middle European, certainly, but at least third-generation American."

"You know, one thing I forgot to ask the Cleveland police. Was he born and raised in Cleveland?"

Salem searched his memory. "No. I seem to remember that he was born in Berkeley, California. I think he first went to reform school there at the age of fourteen. Then I believe the family moved to Chicago for a short time, and on to Cleveland when he was about seventeen or eighteen."

"I don't think you'll find him in Brazil," I said flatly.

He was surprised again. "Why not?"

"Why should he go there? He can't speak the language. He probably wouldn't even enjoy himself there. And it isn't necessary. There are thousands of small towns in America where he could lose himself. Change his appearance just a little, live a law-abiding life, and the odds are against anyone ever uncovering him—especially if he has money."

"You might be right," he said reflectively.

"Well, I won't take up any more of your time," I said. "Thanks for all the cooperation, Mr. Salem."

"You're welcome, but I don't see how any of this can help you." He looked at me sharply. "I've answered your questions, Mr. March. Now answer one for me."

"Sure."

"Twice you've mentioned that you work differently than the regular police. What do you mean by that?"

"Well," I said carefully, "the regular police, even the FBI, have to account to others—superiors, the city, the state, the Federal government, and eventually the public. I don't have to account to anybody or anything, except the laws of this country. I don't have the facilities of the police or the FBI, and I don't usually have much help. And in this case I don't have much time. So I locate the people who seem most obviously involved and I start pushing them. If they're guilty, sooner or later they start making mistakes. When that happens it's only a matter of time until I have my case. You might call it an application of mathematics."

"You might," he said with a smile. "You might also be killed that way."

"That can happen in your bathtub. So far, I've made out. I'm careful—in the bathtub and out."

His gaze flicked across my chest. "You don't seem to be armed."

"I'm not at the moment. But that will be corrected as soon as I return to my hotel."

"Legally?"

I nodded. "I have a gun permit for the District and for a number of states."

"Why will you arm yourself when you get back to the hotel?"

"You wondered why I went to see Johnny Clark. I went to tell him my theory about Thomas Rako and to assure him that I was going to find Rako. I was followed from his building to this one. I expect I'll be followed when I leave here."

"I have a feeling," he said, "that I probably shouldn't ask

any more questions. There may be things I shouldn't know. But I wish you luck. I'd like to see Thomas Rako found. He's a piece of unfinished business in my life."

"I'll try," I told him. "Tell me one more thing. You probably know the Clark organization as well as anyone outside of it. Who would you say are his most important guns?"

"In my opinion," he said carefully, "Thomas Rako was one. There are two more. Jerry Dell here in Washington and Nick Potti who's out in Cleveland."

"I've met both gentlemen."

"He has dozens of assault specialists, but they are his killers. I can't prove it and the police can't prove it, but we all know it."

"I thought that was about the size of it," I said, standing up. "Well, thanks again."

He stood up also and held out his hand. "Don't mention it. Let me know what happens."

"Sure," I said easily.

I turned and walked out of his office. I went downstairs and found a taxi. As it pulled away, I looked through the rear window and saw a sedan pull out from the curb and fall in behind us. There were two people in it. I couldn't see very clearly, but one of them looked like Jerry Dell.

SIX

The taxi let me out in front of the Peraton Hotel. As I went up the steps to where the doorman waited for me, I glanced around and saw the sedan pull into a parking place a half block away. I went on into the lobby, stopping at the desk to see if there was any mail or any calls for me. There weren't.

"I don't suppose you're the night clerk?" I asked the man behind the desk.

"No, sir. He'll be here in about an hour and a half."

"Thanks," I said. I walked across the lobby to the bell captain. He was a short, stocky man who looked to be about thirty-five. I took a ten-dollar bill out of my pocket and folded it so the numerals still showed.

"I'd like to talk to you," I said.

He glanced at the bill and took it all in the same movement. "That's what I'm here for, sir," he said.

"I understand you were working here seven years ago?"

Something in his face changed. "I've been here fourteen years, sir, ten of them as bell captain."

"I wonder if you remember something that happened seven years ago. A man disappeared from this hotel. A man named Thomas Rako."

"Cop?" he asked. His voice sounded more tired than anything else.

"No. Insurance."

"I should've known. Cops don't hand out sawbucks."

"Do you remember him?"

"How could I forget? I've been visited by cops at least four times a year ever since then—just to see if I suddenly remembered something new."

"I don't want you to remember something new," I said. "I just want you to remember something old. I don't know the story, so it'd be new to me. Did you see him come in the day he disappeared?"

"Yes. When I'm here I see everybody come in and go out. Usually I don't know one of them from the other, but his picture was in all the papers, so I knew who he was."

"What happened?"

"Nothing. He came in and stopped at the desk. The clerk went into the office and came back and gave him an envelope."

"Mail?"

"Couldn't have been. That would've been in the box. It must have been something he'd put in the office safe."

"Any idea what it was?"

"No. It was just a plain white envelope."

"What did he do then?"

"Took one of the elevators up. I imagine to his room."

"That's all?"

"That's all."

"Did he come down again?"

"No, sir. That is, I didn't see him. I was here on duty until after midnight."

"Could he have slipped out without your seeing him?"

"Not this way, sir. Not unless he was heavily disguised, and if there had been such a person I would have remembered that."

"Maybe he left after midnight?"

"Perhaps, but everyone who was on duty swore that he did not."

"You said he couldn't have slipped out this way. Is there some other way he could have gone out?"

"There is in every hotel. He could have gone out through the basement. It wouldn't be easy to do without being seen, but I suppose it could be done."

"That's all?"

"That's it. Like I told you, I've said it so often I can repeat it in my sleep."

"Okay. Was Rako carrying anything when he came in that night?"

"Two packages. Looked like clothes."

"All right, thanks," I said.

I went over to the elevators and up to my room. I took off my coat and tie and stretched out on the bed. I was tired. I hadn't realized how tired until I relaxed. I picked up the phone and asked room service to send up a bucket of ice. Then I relaxed some more.

There was a discreet knock on the door. I went over and opened it. The waiter was there with my ice. I let him in and watched him as he put the bucket down in the room and got out the check and a pencil. He seemed to be about fifty-five and had the pale, stooped look of most room-service waiters.

I added a generous tip to the check and signed it. As I handed it to him, he started to turn away, glancing at the tip at the same time. He knew it was too big a tip for just delivering ice. He stopped and looked at me.

"How long have you been working here?" I asked.

"Twenty years, sir."

"That's a long time. Were you on room service seven years ago?"

"Yes, sir."

"Do you remember the man who disappeared from here at that time?"

"I should, sir. I've had to talk about it often enough since."

"How come?"

"I served his last dinner, sir."

"The one he didn't eat?"

"Yes, sir. I've always thought that something must have happened to him right after I left the room."

"The police have kept questioning you all this time?"

"Yes, sir. The police, newspaper reporters, there was even one magazine writer." He said it with pride.

"It must have been quite an experience. Tell me about it."

"What, sir?"

"The night that Mr. Rako disappeared."

"There isn't much to tell," he said sadly. "Mr. Rako called room service and told them what time he wanted his dinner delivered. He asked for me. I had served him the two previous nights. He ordered the same dinner as he had before: rare steak, potatoes, fresh vegetables. One cocktail. Then apple pie and coffee. I brought the dinner up at the time he'd requested. I knocked on the door and he called for me to come in."

"He was here then?" I asked. I'd been harboring the idea that he might have gone earlier and had ordered the dinner to make it seem as though he were still around.

"Yes, sir. I wheeled the table in and set it up. He called out to tell me that there was money on the dresser and to keep the change."

"Called out? Where was he?"

"In the bathroom. Taking a shower, I believe. The door was partly open and I could hear the shower."

"Did he always pay in cash instead of signing the check?"

"No, sir. I guess he knew he would be in the shower and didn't want to have to come out to sign the check."

"What did you do then?"

"Picked up the money and left. But do you know how much it was?"

"How much?"

"A hundred-dollar bill. That was the largest tip I ever received in thirty years as a waiter."

"I guess he must have felt in a generous mood," I said. "What else?"

"That's all, sir. I never saw him again."

I was tempted to point out that he hadn't seen him that time either, but I refrained. "Well, thank you."

"Yes, sir," he said. He went to the door, then looked back. "I read everything that the newspapers said about Mr. Rako. Maybe they were true, but as far as I was concerned, he was a gentleman."

"He made sure of that, I guess," I said. "Thanks."

He took the hint and left. As soon as he was gone, I put ice in a glass and poured a very generous portion of whiskey into it. I slipped my shoes off, fluffed up the pillows on the bed, and stretched out. I lit a cigarette and made a sample testing of the whiskey. Everything was just about right—for the minute.

I'd been so busy since the case had been handed to me the morning before that there'd been no time really to think about it. As soon as I was relaxed and the whiskey was building a pleasant fire in my stomach, I started thinking.

I had to start someplace. The more I thought about it, the better I liked the idea that Johnny Clark had helped Rako get away and reach a hiding place. It made sense from almost every angle. Especially now. If Clark knew that Rako was dead, he wouldn't bother having his men follow me. Now, even if I found a body, it would be pretty hard to prove who had murdered Rako. How right I was would depend to some degree on how long they continued to follow me. If they stayed on the trail, it could be pretty good proof that Rako was alive somewhere, that Clark either knew where he was or wanted to learn, and that when I either got too close or found him, they'd act. On the other hand, if he knew where Rako was, he might act as soon as he thought I was on the right track.

All right, I told myself, I had a theory. The next question was how it worked. How had Rako gotten out of the hotel and to some sort of transportation without being recognized? His picture had been in all the newspapers at the time and somebody should have recognized him.

Then I realized there was an easy answer to one part of that question. Newspaper photographs are not noted for their brilliant clarity. I was remembering the picture I'd seen in the newspaper in Cleveland. Rako had been wearing a snap-brimmed hat and had been trying to duck the cameraman. Put the same man in a cap and a different type of suit, make a few minor changes in his face—maybe shave off part of his eyebrows, even pad his cheeks a little—and probably no one would take a second look unless they knew the police were looking for him. That was no great problem.

I was sure that the FBI had done a thorough job of checking all exit points from Washington. But there were two factors that might have foiled their investigation. He could have left by car, and there wouldn't have been any way to check it. But somehow I doubted if he had done so. It would have been too slow for a man in a hurry.

Then there was a time element. According to the testimony of the room-service waiter, the time Rako had left was more or less fixed. He'd arrived at the hotel at about five-thirty and he hadn't left until sometime after his dinner was served, which was—I suddenly sat up on the bed. I must have been tired. I'd slipped up.

I picked up the phone and asked for room service. "This is Room 1091," I said when they answered. "I'd like a pot of coffee, and would you please send it up with the same waiter who brought me ice about a half hour ago?"

"Yes, sir," a voice said with an inflection that implied it was accustomed to answering the requests of nuts.

I remained in a sitting position and waited, pouring myself

another drink in the meantime. It was about ten minutes before the knock came on the door.

"Come in," I called.

The door opened and the waiter entered with the coffee. He put it down and handed me the check.

"Aren't you going to have dinner, sir?" he asked.

"Later," I said. I added another generous tip and gave him the check. "What's your name?"

"Herman, sir."

"All right, Herman, do you remember what time you brought dinner to Mr. Rako that night seven years ago?"

"Yes, sir. It was the same time he'd ordered it delivered the other two nights. Seven-thirty."

"Fine. Now, will you do me a favor?"

"If I can, sir."

"You can."

I got up and walked into the bathroom. I turned both faucets of the shower on and came back to the room. I swung the bathroom door half shut.

"Was that about the way the door was that night when you brought the dinner?"

"I think so, sir."

"Now, would you go out into the corridor, close the door, and then knock on it?"

He looked puzzled, but he started out of the room. I went into the bathroom and swung the door to the same position as before. I waited while I counted to thirty slowly. I heard nothing. I went out and opened the door. The waiter was standing there.

"Did you knock?" I asked him.

"Yes, sir. Twice."

"Thank you, Herman. That's all."

I closed the door and went back to the bed and my drink.

So the record showed that Thomas Rako had arrived at the hotel at about five-thirty and didn't leave until shortly after seven-thirty. But suppose he'd really come back to the hotel and left, say, fifteen minutes later. He should have been able to change clothes and alter his appearance slightly in that length of time. And it would have given him almost two hours during which everyone would think he was still in the hotel.

All he would have needed was a little help. Someone who came up to his room and waited. Someone who turned on the shower slightly before seven-thirty, the time the dinner had been ordered, then put a hundred-dollar bill on the dresser. Someone who had waited just inside the room until the knock came, called for the waiter to come in, then stepped inside the bathroom out of sight and called out to tell the waiter the money was on the dresser and to keep the change. No waiter would have thought anything of this normally, but with a hundred dollars staring him in the face he'd think even less. Then the man, whoever he was, would slip out of the room, wipe the doorknob with his handkerchief, and leave the hotel without anyone paying any attention to him.

It could have worked that way. Maybe it did and maybe it didn't, but it was a starting place.

Reluctantly, I sat up on the bed. I put on my shoes, then my tie and coat. I made sure I had my key and left the room. I walked down past the bank of elevators and opened the door to the stairs. I walked down the ten flights to the basement and stepped out into it.

I made a few false starts before I got my bearings and headed for the rear of the hotel. I saw two employees as I went along the corridor, but they paid no attention to me.

It looked like clear sailing and then I came to the exit. There was a man there, sitting on a stool, wearing a gray uniform with the name of the hotel stitched on the pocket. He looked up as he heard my footsteps.

"Sorry," he said as I reached him, "you must have lost your way. Are you a guest?"

Funny how sometimes you think you've found an easy answer to something and then find there's a perfectly simple factor you've overlooked.

"Yes," I said. "I'm in Room 1091. I thought I'd like to take a look at the basement."

"Sorry, sir," he said politely, "but guests are not permitted down here. I'm surprised the elevator operator didn't tell you."

"I walked down," I admitted. "Is there someone on duty at this door all the time?"

"Twenty-four hours a day."

"What if I wanted to go out the back and take a walk?"

He shook his head, smiling. "Not permitted, sir. There's really nothing to see back there anyway. ... Would you mind stepping to one side, sir, so these men can get out?"

I stepped to the wall and looked around. Two men in white uniforms walked by carrying a huge, oblong basket piled high with crumpled linens. It looked as if it weighed a good two hundred pounds. The guard opened the door for them and they passed through.

"What's that?" I asked.

"Hotel laundry."

"But I thought there was a laundry here in the hotel?"

"Yes, sir, there is. A small laundry used for the guests, but the hotel things go out to a commercial laundry."

"Which one?"

"Martinson. They're one of the best."

"Have they been doing the hotel laundry long?"

"Years."

"How long have you been here?"

"Six years." He was looking at me curiously. "You did say you were a guest, sir?"

"Yes. Why?"

He hesitated. "Well, guests usually don't ask so many questions."

"I'm a writer," I said. "I guess I'm just naturally curious about how things work. Sorry I bothered you."

"That's all right, sir," he said, but I had a feeling he was watching me as I walked away. I found the stairway door and walked up to the main floor. I took an elevator the rest of the way.

I was barely in the room when the phone rang. I picked it up and answered.

"Mr. March?" a man's voice asked.

"Yes."

"Sorry to bother you, Mr. March. This is the hotel's security officer. Were you just down in the basement?"

"Yes, I was. I was curious about what it was like down there. I didn't realize it was against the rules."

"It's not that. We just don't encourage guests to go there. Too many of them would interfere with the work of the employees. I just wanted to check with you to be sure there wasn't a prowler posing as one of the guests. Good night, sir." He hung up.

I took off my coat, tie, and shoes and went back to my favorite position. For a moment in the basement I'd been afraid that one small part of my theory was out the window. But the sight of the laundry men had given me a fresh idea.

I decided I was hungry. I called room service and told them to send up a double martini, a rare steak with all the trimmings, and a big pot of coffee. I said that I'd like to have Herman bring it. I hung up and went into the bathroom. I splashed cold water on my face and felt a little better, but I was still just as tired. I went back, lit a cigarette, and waited.

It wasn't long before there was a knock on the door and Herman wheeled the table in. I had him leave the steak and vegetables covered so they'd stay hot while I finished my drink. I added a tip to the check and signed it. Herman hesitated, as though he thought I wanted to ask him more questions, but left when he saw that I had no such intention.

I drank my martini slowly and enjoyed every minute of it. When I'd finished, I had a good appetite for the steak. I had coffee and began to feel that life was good after all. I turned on the TV set and watched a show that didn't tax my attention too much.

Herman stopped by for the table and dishes shortly after

nine. I got undressed and climbed into bed. The sheets felt great, the way they do only when you're very tired. There was a comedy show on TV. It wasn't very good, but it didn't tax my mind to watch it, and I needed that kind of rest, too. I had a V.O. on the rocks and another cigarette and waited for the time to come when I wouldn't be able to keep my eyes open.

The telephone rang. I picked it up.

"Milo?" a hearty voice said. I thought I recognized it, but waited to see. "This is Johnny Clark." I'd been right.

"That's nice," I said.

"I called to apologize for blowing my top this afternoon. I'd had a hard day, but that was no reason why I should've taken it out on you."

"That's all right. How did you know where to find me?"

"Oh, I called around town until I got the hotel where you're staying."

"You mean," I said, "that one of your boys called from a pay phone and told you where I'd holed up. Are they still outside waiting for me? If so, you might as well let them off the hook. I'm already in bed. But I may go out early in the morning."

He laughed. "I told you I like sharp guys. I hear you paid a visit to Bob Salem this afternoon."

"I thought you'd hear about it."

"That must've been quite a meeting. How is the boy wonder?"

"Still wondering how you get away with it," I said.

"Say, Milo, what are you doing in bed this time of day? It's not even ten o'clock yet. Come on out and I'll show you our town."

"I've seen your town," I said. "Besides, I'm tired. I saw Cleveland last night. And tomorrow's going to be a busy day."

"Oh, yes, I forgot. You're going to find our Tom. How are you making out?"

"I'm satisfied so far," I said. I decided to push him a little more. "I think Rako left the hotel almost two hours earlier than everyone figured, while a friend stayed in his room. Even that could be quite an advantage when the authorities started checking airlines and other means of transportation. Then, other friends helped him to get out of the hotel without being seen."

"That's a lot of help. Where would a man find that many friends to help him?"

"How many men work for you in the Carrier Workers?" I asked.

There was a moment of silence, then he laughed again. "Still on that, huh? I like you, Milo. I don't know why, but I do. You're my kind of man. How much money do you make?"

"I don't even tell Internal Revenue that."

"You're the kind of man I always need. How'd you like to come to work for me? You could make twenty, thirty thousand a year right away."

"I make more than that now. In fact, I expect to make more than that on this one case. What are you so nervous about, Johnny? Did I draw blood this afternoon?"

Again there was a silence, and when he spoke, the laughter was gone and his voice was grim. "I had nothing to do with Tom Rako's disappearance, but you've decided to get on my back about it. I've got enough lousy cops on my back. I'm tired of it, that's all. Just get off."

"I'll remember to bring a padded saddle."

"Don't push your luck too far, March," he said harshly. "I can play rough, too—if I have to."

"I'll bet you can—and have."

"All right," he said abruptly. "It's on your head."

"It always has been. But thanks for calling. I think it's relaxed me enough so I can go to sleep."

He swore and hung up. I padded across the room, turned off the TV, and went back to bed. When I'd finished my drink, I put out my cigarette and turned off the light. I was asleep almost before the room got dark.

I was up early the next morning, though, feeling like a new man. I ordered breakfast from room service and took a fast shower while it was being delivered.

After breakfast I shaved and got dressed. Then I went downstairs and the doorman called a cab for me.

As the taxi pulled away, I looked behind me. Sure enough, there was that same sedan falling into line. I smiled to myself. I wondered how Jerry Dell liked getting up so early.

The first stop was at the Martinson Laundry Company. I patiently went from person to person until I finally ended up with the manager. His name was Pearson. I showed him my identification and told him who I was working for. He looked unhappy.

"I don't understand," he said. "This is not the company we're insured with, and I'm positive that everything about our insurance is in order."

"Who does carry your insurance?" I asked.

"Well, the insurance on our employees is with Interstate

Workers and the insurance on our plant and equipment is with Monig Mutual, but we're very happy with both companies and have no desire to change."

"I'm not selling insurance," I told him. "This is a matter of cooperation between insurance companies. I'd like some information from your records about your contract with the Peraton Hotel."

His manner changed. "I'm afraid that's quite impossible. We can't open our records to just anyone who comes in off the street. As far as I know, you might be sent here by one of our competitors."

I pulled money from my pocket. "I realize that your time is valuable ..."

"No," he said curtly. "Our records are not for sale either. I'm afraid that I must ask you to leave, Mr. March."

"It's refreshing to meet an honest man," I told him. I put the money back in my pocket. "I don't suppose you'd mind telling me what union your pickup men belong to?"

"Carrier Workers," he said. "Now, if you'll just leave."

"Sure," I said. "But I'll be back."

"It'll be a waste of time, yours and mine."

"I'll remember that," I told him.

I went out and hailed a cab. I had it take me back to the hotel. The sedan followed. I went upstairs and put in a call to Martin Raymond in New York. He was on the phone as soon as he learned who it was.

"Milo," he said. "Got the case all solved?"

"You're an optimistic one," I said. "I need a little help. Know anybody at Interstate Workers Insurance or at Monig Mutual?"

"Interstate," he said, "is a company owned entirely by officers of the Carrier Workers union. Their main office is in St. Louis. I've never had any dealings with them. Monig is a legitimate company. The head office is here in New York, and I know most of their people quite well. What do you want?"

"There's a Martinson Laundry Company here in Washington. Monig carries the insurance on their plant and equipment. I want some information from their records. The manager of the place refused to give it to me this morning, so I thought maybe you could bring a little pressure on him through his insurance company."

"I'll see what I can do," he said. "Where are you?"

"Peraton Hotel in Washington."

"I'll call you back," he said, and broke the connection.

I poured myself a drink and waited.

It was a little more than a half hour before Raymond called back.

"Milo," he said, when I answered the phone, "they'll do it. Ranson at Monig owes me a couple of favors. He checked the records on the company while I was on the phone and discovered they've collected on several claims. He's calling the manager and suggesting it would be better if he cooperated. Better give it an hour or so in the event he doesn't get through on the first call."

"Thanks, Martin."

"Anything for the old teamwork. How's it coming, Milo?"

"Pretty good, I think. I'll let you know." I hung up.

I went downstairs, bought a newspaper in the lobby, and went into the bar. I had a long, leisurely drink while I read the paper and then the hour was up. I went out and got a cab, directing the driver back to the laundry company. The boys in the sedan fell in behind it. When we reached the laundry I went in and soon found the manager. He didn't look too pleased to see me.

"I've been instructed to cooperate with you," he said sourly.

"I thought you might be," I said. "How long do you keep your records?"

"The policy is not to throw out any customer records until they are at least fifteen years old."

"How often do you pick up laundry from the Peraton?"

"Three times a week."

"How long has this been true?"

"I think since the beginning of the contract, Mr. March."

"Can you tell me if you picked up laundry at the Peraton on May 6th seven years ago?"

He looked startled. "Seven years ago? I'll have to check the records on that."

He picked up the telephone and pushed a button. "Miss Weymouth, would you please bring me the records on the Peraton Hotel for seven years ago? Yes, that is correct." He put the phone down and looked at me. "Mr. March, if you'd please tell me what this is about, I'd appreciate it."

"It isn't anything that involves your company," I told him. "I prefer not to tell you what I'm looking for at the moment, but you can relax. I'm not investigating you at all. But I think that you may have information that will help me."

He slid down in his chair and stared moodily at the desk. I couldn't help wondering if there might not be something wrong with his insurance since he was so nervous, but I didn't say anything, and we waited in silence until an attractive redhead came in with a huge folder. She put the folder on the desk and left. He started thumbing through it and finally stopped.

"You said May 6th?"

"Yes."

"There was a pickup at the hotel on the evening of that date."

"Are the men who made the pickup still working for you?"

"I don't know," he said. He glanced at the folder again and lifted the receiver of his phone. "Bring me the cards on two employees named Jablonsky and Minetti, Adam and Anthony."

Again we waited. The girl came in with two more folders and placed them in front of him. He opened them and looked at the contents. Finally his gaze lifted to meet mine.

"They were both fired on May 7th of that same year."

"Why?"

"They had five more commercial pickups to make after the Peraton. They didn't make any of them and refused to tell us where they'd been all that time, so they were fired."

"No fuss from the union?"

"There doesn't seem to have been any. The report merely indicates that that union agreed with us, and sent over two men to replace them."

"Could I have the addresses of the guys you fired?"

"I guess so." He took a sheet of paper from the desk drawer and copied the names and addresses, then pushed it across to me. "They may not live there now."

"I'll find them," I said. I stood up. "Thanks for the help."

"What's it all about?" he asked again.

"A man who disappeared," I said. I smiled at him. "You've been a big help. Good-bye." I turned and left before he could ask any more questions.

Down in the street I stopped at the curb and looked for a taxi. I heard approaching footsteps and looked around. Jerry Dell had gotten out of the sedan and was coming up to me.

"What were you doing in there?" he asked abruptly.

"You know how it is," I said. "I have a couple of dirty shirts and I wanted to see if they'd do them for me."

"I hate wise guys. That's a union shop, our union. You trying to louse us up?"

"I couldn't do that, Jerry," I said evenly. "You're already about as lousy as they come."

He stared at me and that strange glow was back in his eyes. Then he glanced around the street and his gaze came back to me.

"What's wrong, Jerry?" I asked. "Too many witnesses?"

"Someday," he said, pushing the words through his clenched teeth, "you and me are going to get together, March. Someday, baby."

"Sure. In the meantime just stay away from me. I've seen too many guys like you—on slabs."

I saw a taxi and waved. It swerved into the curb.

"Just a minute, March," Jerry Dell said. He put his hand on my arm as I reached for the door. "I ain't finished talking to you yet."

"You were finished before you even started," I said. "Get your hand off my arm."

His lips stretched in what was supposed to be a smile. "Make me," he said.

"With pleasure."

I swung a short left into his midriff. It wasn't hard enough to do any real damage, but it made him stagger back. I swung around and hit him with a hard right to the jaw. He went sprawling across the sidewalk. I opened the door of the cab and climbed in. The driver started up without waiting to ask me where I wanted to go.

SEVEN

As the cab pulled away I turned and looked through the rear window. Jerry Dell was on the sidewalk, propped up on one elbow. For a minute it looked as if he were going to pull his gun. His right hand was already groping beneath his coat. Then he must have realized it was too dangerous. His hand slowly came into sight again and he got to his feet. He hurried to the sedan and they took off after us.

The driver must have been watching in his rearview mirror. "He's following us," he said nervously. "What is this, mister?"

"Don't worry," I told him. "They won't do anything now. They've been following me since yesterday. They won't do any more—now."

"You're sure, mister? I've got a wife and kids. Maybe we ought to stop the first cop we come to."

"It wouldn't do any good. Anyway, when they try to do anything to me, it won't be out in the open like this."

"Okay, mister. Where to?"

I thought for a minute. "You'd better take me to the Pera-ton Hotel first."

"Okay. ... Say, that was a beautiful right, mister. A little bit harder and they'da been counting over him."

"I didn't want to knock him out. I just wanted to hurt him a little, mostly in the ego."

He drove in silence for a couple of minutes. "It's none of my business, mister," he said then, "but what was that about?"

"What union do you belong to?" I asked.

"Drivers Union. Why?" He sounded puzzled.

"Ever hear of the Carrier Workers union?"

"That bunch of gangsters! They been trying to take us over for the last five years. What's that got to do with it?"

"The man I knocked down is one of the hoods who works for the Carrier Workers."

"You should've hit him harder! How come he's following you?"

"I'm trying to pin something on his union leader," I said. "He's following me to see where I go and what I do."

"You some kind of cop?"

"Some kind."

"Then I'm with you, mister. I got a handy lug wrench up here in front, and if we need help I can get a dozen cabbies on the radiophone."

"I don't think we'll need them," I said, "but thanks." When we reached the hotel I paid him for what was on the meter but asked him to wait. He said he would and I went upstairs. I'd decided that I'd pushed Jerry Dell enough to have to take out some insurance.

Up in the room I checked my gun permit to make sure that it was still valid. I took the shoulder holster from my suitcase and strapped it on. I checked the .38 and slipped it into the holster. I put a box of shells in my pocket and went back down to the street. The driver was still waiting. I climbed in and gave him the address I had for Adam Jablonsky. The sedan was following as we pulled away from the curb.

It was a working-class neighborhood filled with apartment buildings, all dingy and looking alike. I had the driver wait and I went looking. There was a Jablonsky on the third floor of one building. I walked up some stairs and rang the bell. After a moment the apartment door opened and an old woman looked out.

"I'm looking for Adam Jablonsky," I said. "Does he live here?"

"He used to live here," she said. She had a slight accent.

"I wonder if you could tell me where I could find him? Are you his mother?"

"I was his mother, yes."

"I don't understand. Aren't you still his mother?"

"My son is dead, mister—almost seven years now."

"Seven years?"

She nodded. "It was May 12th. Two sons and a husband—all gone. There's just me, mister."

"I'm sorry to hear about it, Mrs. Jablonsky. How did it happen?"

"He was going to look for a job. He'd just lost his other job and he had a meeting about a new one. He said it was going to be a better job. He was feeling so good. I watched from the window as he left, such a fine, big man, just like his papa. Then, as he crossed the street, there is this car. It comes like the driver is crazy, maybe drunk. It hits my son and then goes on like maybe he only ran over a little bug in the street."

"Did you get a good look at the car or the driver?"

"The car is like any car, mister. They all look alike. I no see anything except my son in the street. He was dead when I got to him. There wasn't even time to get a priest."

"What did the police say?"

"They say he is dead. They say they look for the car, but they never find it. What do they care? He is not their son. They do not carry him inside the body for nine months and then inside the heart for twenty-five years."

"I'm sorry, Mrs. Jablonsky," I said. "And I'm sorry I revived the memory."

"You do not forget a son, mister," she said, but she wasn't looking at me. She was staring through me at some ghost which only she could see.

I said good-bye and went downstairs. The taxi was still waiting. So was the sedan, a half block away. I gave the driver the next address and settled back in the seat.

I wasn't so lucky on the next one. The Minettis had moved, and no one seemed to know where they'd gone. They weren't listed in the phone book. Then I tried the neighborhood stores. It was the druggist who came up with something. He thought that Mrs. Minetti had returned to his store to fill a prescription sometime after she'd moved. He dug around in the back of the store until he found the prescription, and then gave me an address that was about ten blocks away.

It was an old, run-down building. I walked up to the fifth floor and found the door with *Minetti* on it. I knocked on it.

The door was opened by a small, dark-haired woman still in her early thirties. She must have been very pretty once, but now she looked gaunt and tired.

"Mrs. Minetti?" I asked.

She nodded.

"I'd like to talk to your husband, Anthony. Is he home?"

"My husband is dead."

"I'm sorry," I said. "When did this happen?"

"Seven years ago. In May. Then there was just me and the three kids. Little Tony was only one. He doesn't even remember his father."

"How did it happen?"

"Tony had just lost his job," she said dully. "He went down the street to a bar to see if some of the fellows knew where he could get another job. He got in a fight with some man there and the man killed him. Tony wasn't a drinking man. He was there because he wanted a job to support his children."

"Was it somebody he knew?"

She shook her head. "Everybody said the man was a stranger and he picked the fight with Tony. A friend of Tony's told me about it. The man picked a fight with Tony and knocked him down. Then he grabbed a bottle from the bar, broke it, and jammed the broken end into Tony's throat." Her face paled as she spoke. "That's what the police said and that's what Tony's friend said. Did you know Tony?"

"No. I wish I had."

"He was a good man. He didn't drink and he didn't chase around with other women. He was a good father. He worked hard for us. Why would some man come out of nowhere and do something like that to him? I light candles every day and ask that question, but I never get an answer."

"I don't know," I said gently, which wasn't quite true. I thought I had a pretty good answer. "What did the police find out?"

"Nothing."

"You mean they didn't find the killer?"

She shook her head. "He ran out right after he did it. Everybody in the bar described him the best they could, but the police were never able to find him."

"It must have been rough for you the last seven years," I said. "How have you managed?"

"I have part-time work. And Tony's union has given me money almost every week."

Blood money, I thought. "Well, thanks, Mrs. Minetti. I'm sorry about your husband."

"What did you want to see him about?"

"I was hoping he could give me some information. Goodbye, Mrs. Minetti." I turned and went down the stairs.

When I got in the taxi I told the driver to wait a few minutes. I leaned back and went over what I'd learned. I always had enough trouble swallowing one coincidence; two was more than I could manage.

Jablonsky and Minetti had both died within a week after losing their jobs for not making any calls after their stop at the Peraton Hotel. There was only one conclusion to draw. Rako had managed to leave the hotel without being seen because he'd gone out in a laundry basket. Then the two drivers had taken him somewhere, which was why they hadn't been able to make their other pickups.

The chief question was, where had they taken him? The reason they had, I thought, was clear. They were members of the Carrier Workers union, while taxi drivers were not. And they had been the only witnesses to where Rako had gone. Like a lot of other witnesses, they had died shortly thereafter.

They must have taken him to the airport. Where had he gone after that? Assuming that he had an ultimate destination picked out, I doubted if he'd head directly for it. He'd go somewhere else first—maybe a couple of places—in order to confuse the trail. I was also assuming that he'd partially disguised himself and that he used a different name. I was sure that the FBI had been as thorough as they always were, but there certainly hadn't been much to start with. I didn't have much choice. I had to make two guesses and then pray that they were right—maybe three guesses.

Guess number one, I told myself, crossing my fingers: Rako had originally come from Berkeley, California. Maybe he would head first for San Francisco, which he must know and where he might have some contacts aside from the union. It was also a large enough city to help in confusing a trail. I hoped I was right. I had one contact there that might be invaluable.

Guess number two: He'd caught a plane that left between five-thirty and seven-thirty in the evening. A situation had been created, if my earlier guess was right, to make everyone think that he'd left not later than seven-thirty. This would have been done only because he planned on leaving before that.

There was another part to this guess: He must not have planned on running out very far in advance of his doing it. If he had, he would've left even before the hearings started. Salem had said that Rako and Johnny Clark lunched the day of the hearing, and also that the seventy-five thousand dollars had been drawn out of the bank immediately after that lunch. So the disappearance must have been planned then. It had been planned carefully, so I doubted that Rako had even called up and made a reservation with an airline. That could also have been traced.

I checked my watch. I still had time before my luncheon appointment. I told the cab driver to take me back to the section where the Minettis had formerly lived. When we got there I soon found the local bar. We stopped in front of it.

"Keep the flag down," I said. "You want to come in and have a drink?"

He glanced back at the sedan, which had parked about a half block away. "I guess I could go a beer," he said.

We went inside. I threw a five-dollar bill on the bar. "Give me a double V.O.," I said, "and my friend here whatever he wants." I turned and went to the phone booth and called the information number at the airport. "I'd like to get some information," I said when the girl answered, "about flights out of Washington seven years ago."

"Just a minute," she said. She sounded puzzled.

It was more than a minute, but finally a man answered. "What was it you wanted?" he asked.

"My name is March," I said. "I'm with the Intercontinental Insurance Company out of New York. I'd like some information on flights out of Washington seven years ago."

"I'm sorry," he said coldly, "but we can't give out any information from the records over the phone. I suggest that you write us a letter and then we can make a decision about it."

"But … ," I began.

"That is our firm policy," he said curtly. There was a click as he disconnected.

I replaced the receiver and left the booth.

The taxi driver was at the bar, working on his beer. My glass of V.O. was waiting for me beside my change. I took a drink and glanced at the bartender. He looked as if he'd been tending bar a long time. I called him over and separated one dollar from the rest of the change. I pushed it across the bar.

"For your piggy bank," I said.

He took the bill without saying anything and put it in a glass back of the bar. He turned back to stare at me impassively.

"Been working here long?" I asked.

"Twenty years. My brother-in-law owns the joint."

"Is this the bar where Tony Minetti was killed seven years ago?"

He hesitated. "Yeah, it happened here. But we was in the clear. The ABC looked it over and said so."

"I believe you," I said. "I just suddenly remembered that it happened in a neighborhood bar and thought maybe this was it."

"Were you a friend of Tony's?" he asked.

"Yeah, I just came from seeing his wife," I said, and hoped that seemed to answer the question. "I've been away for seven years. Were you on the stick that night?"

"I was here."

"A terrible thing," I said. "The way I heard it, Tony never had a chance. It must've happened fast."

"You can say that again," he told me. "Tony was here having a beer at the bar with some of his friends. Tony was a nice guy, you know, a two- or three-beer man and never no trouble. Then this other guy came in. I spotted him for a hood the minute he came through the door, but he was sober and there wasn't no reason I could refuse to serve him. He had a couple of fast drinks and I guess he must've got juiced up even though he didn't show it. He made a crack to Tony. Tony turned around, a little hot, and answered it. The guy hit him and Tony was on the floor. The guy grabbed a bottle off the bar, smashed the end off it, and dived on top of Tony. The whole thing was over before I could even grab my club from under the bar. And the guy beat it. The whole thing was maybe no more than two, three minutes. Just like that and a nice guy is dead."

"You got a good look at the hood?"

"I got a good look at him, but that didn't keep him from getting away. Some of the customers rushed out after him and so did I. All we saw then was a taillight pulling away, and it was already too far to see the license plate."

"How come the bottle was on the table?"

"The guy asked me to leave it there."

I nodded. "And the cops never caught up with the guy?"

"No, but somebody else did."

"What do you mean?"

"I guess it was a couple of months later," he said. "One of the detectives came in and asked me to go down and look at a guy in the morgue. He'd been fished out of the river. Well, he was the guy, all right. But he was good and dead. The detective told me he was a small-time hood, but they couldn't connect him with anybody. They figured out that maybe he was hopped up that night and just felt like killing somebody. You know how those hopheads are."

"Sure," I said. I shook my head. "Never know how it's going to happen, do we?"

"You can say that again, brother. And Tony was a swell guy."

"That's right. Remember what the name of the hood was?"

"Sure. A funny name. Willie Nemo."

"Just some punk," I said, shaking my head again. I finished my drink and put the change in my pocket. "Well, I'll see you around."

"Sure," he said, and walked off.

I nodded to the taxi driver and we went out to the cab. It was about time for lunch.

"Know where the Lido Restaurant is?" I asked.

"Yes."

"Let's go."

We pulled out and the sedan followed faithfully. "It ain't none of my business, mister," the driver said, "but was that part of it, too?"

"That was part of it."

"The Carrier Workers?"

"I think so, but I can't prove it. Forget what I told you."

It was certainly part of it, I told myself. Three men dead— just so that one man could run away from a Congressional probe. And there might be even more.

We arrived at the Lido at just about the right time. I paid

the driver the meter sum and gave him an extra-large tip. He'd stuck by me even when he was scared, so he'd earned it.

"If you want me to, I can stick around," he said. "I mean without the meter running."

I glanced at his license. "No thanks, Irving. If I need you, I'll call your company. Thanks for everything."

"I hope it works out," he said fervently. "I can't stand them rats."

I thanked him again and went into the restaurant. I told the waiter that I was joining Mr. Macklin. He took me to a table in one of the corners in back. George Macklin was already there. He looked much as I remembered him. We shook hands and I sat down.

"I seem to remember that you drank martinis," he said. "Is it still the same?"

"I'll go along with it," I said with a smile.

He gave the order to the waiter and we traded small talk until after the drinks were delivered. I tried mine. It was a good martini.

"Do you have any contacts in the police department?" I asked.

"After twenty years as a Washington columnist? Want somebody arrested?"

"Yes—and no. Just seven years ago there was a laundry worker named Anthony Minetti killed in what was supposed to be a barroom brawl. Not much later a small-time hood named Willie Nemo was pulled out of the river, a murder victim. He was identified as the man who had killed Minetti. I'd like to know what happened about the case."

"Just a minute," he said.

He got up and left the table. I turned my full attention to the martini. It was finished and I'd already ordered another before George Macklin returned.

He slipped into his seat just as the waiter brought the second round. He didn't say anything until the waiter left, but I could see that he thought he was on a story and wasn't interested in other things.

"Not much to know," he said when the waiter was gone. "Nemo was killed by person or persons unknown. The case is still open. Nemo was really small time. He had no friends and was not a part of any gang. Nobody has the slightest idea why he was killed—nor why he killed Minetti. The police could find no connection between the two men." He waited a second. "What's it all about, March?"

I took a long drink before I answered. "Most of it will have to be off the record for the present. But when the time is right, it's your story."

"That's the story of my life," he said with a sigh. "But I'll go along with it, as I always do. Is it a good story?"

"It is—if I'm right. And I think I am. Remember the name Thomas Rako?"

"Sure," he said, his eyes brightening. "You got something about him?"

"I think so. I was handed the case two days ago by my insurance company. But I don't have much time. In thirty days the courts can declare Rako legally dead and there's a million dollars in insurance to be paid out. With only a month to work on it, there was no time for orthodox methods. Besides, they had already been used for almost seven years with no luck. So I tried guessing what had happened."

"Clark and the Carrier Workers?"

I nodded. "I got action on that right away. I tried it in Cleveland and I suddenly became about as popular as Barry Goldwater at a Communist rally. When I arrived in Washington I went to see Johnny Clark. He was expecting me. I told him my ideas. He didn't care for them. His reaction might have been normal for an innocent man, but what happened later wasn't. When I left his office he sent two of his trained seals to follow me. They're still with me, somewhere outside."

"Who're the two men?"

"One is Jerry Dell. I don't know who the other is. I had a small altercation with Dell this morning and knocked him down."

"I noticed you were carrying a gun," he said dryly. "It's a wise move. Dell is a tough baby. He was a contract killer for the syndicate before he went to work for Clark, but nobody's pinned anything on him since he was arrested for carrying a gun at the age of sixteen. You have anything else?"

"I think so. The theory has always been that Rako was fixed at the hotel until seven-thirty when his dinner was delivered. I say that he left the hotel voluntarily shortly after five-thirty."

"But there was testimony about that. I remember. I covered the whole case because it involved Clark."

"Sure. There was one witness—the waiter who brought the dinner. He says, and believes, that Rako was there, told him to come in, paid for the dinner, and gave him the biggest tip he's ever had in his life. But it wasn't Rako. It was somebody else."

"How do you arrive at that?"

"Rako was supposedly taking a shower with the door partly open when the waiter arrived. The waiter knocked and Rako called out to him to come in; then told him there was money on the dresser and to take it and keep the change. There's only one thing wrong with the story. You can turn on the shower in those bathrooms and stand inside with the door partly open and you can't hear a knock on the outside door. So whoever was there had to wait in the room until the knock came, call out for the waiter to come in, and then duck out of sight in the bathroom. From there, he called out the rest of the instructions. There was a hundred-dollar bill on the dresser and the waiter was told to keep the change. With a C-note staring him in the face, the waiter wasn't thinking too carefully about anything else. He's sure it was Rako he was talking to, but he didn't see him, and I doubt if anyone could positively identify a voice when that shower is running. It gave Rako almost two hours' extra time."

"Does anybody else know this?"

"They may. I don't know. Most law enforcement bodies don't care too much for cooperating with insurance detectives."

"Well, it's an interesting point. Do you have anything else? I seem to remember that there was some question about how Rako got out of the hotel without being noticed."

"I have an idea about that, too," I said. "I think he went out through the basement."

He considered that for a minute, then snapped his fingers. "I knew there was something about that. I remember it now.

There was a guard on duty at the exit from the basement. Placed there, I believe, to keep the employees from walking out with hotel property. You think they bought him?"

"No. They didn't have to. There was a pickup that night of the hotel laundry. It's carried out in huge baskets, large enough for a man to be concealed under the laundry. The laundry men were members of the Carrier Workers union. The two men didn't make the other stops they were supposed to make that day and were both fired the following day."

"That sounds like something," he said excitedly. "How did you dig that up?"

"Luck. The rest was just following it up. But that's only part of it. The two men, Adam Jablonsky and Anthony Minetti, were both accidentally killed within the next week. I don't believe in accidents."

"Just a minute," he said. He wrote down the two names.

"Jablonsky was killed by a hit-and-run driver who was never caught. Minetti was killed by Willie Nemo—who was then fished out of the river. At least three men dead just so Thomas Rako could step off into the wild blue yonder."

"And it ties in with Johnny Clark? Do you think you can prove that?"

"Not unless I find Rako. He's the one with all the proof, I think."

"What does that mean?"

"Rako came up in Clark's organization very fast. In fact, I believe he's the only one ever to become a business partner of Clark's—through their two wives. And there were several tougher and more experienced rough boys already working for Clark. My theory is that Rako had something on Clark.

Then Rako was considered the key witness in the Congressional hearings and there was a chance he might break. He had been an informer when he was in prison. I don't think Clark would have let him live—unless he had to. I think that Rako still has whatever he had on Clark, and that Clark helped him to get away and has probably been supporting him with union funds."

"You told this to Clark?"

"Yes. I've been followed since then. I think that indicates I'm on the right track."

"Sounds like it," he said. He chewed absent-mindedly on his pencil. "What can I do?"

"Most of it's up to me," I said. "But I want a photograph of Rako, the most recent one, which would be one taken at the hearing. And I'd prefer one that really showed his face. Maybe your paper has one."

"That shouldn't be any problem. How long are you staying in Washington?"

"I hope I'll leave tonight."

"I'll send a picture over to your hotel this afternoon. I'm not going directly back to the paper, but you should have it by three or four. Will that be all right?"

"Fine."

"What else?"

"I don't think I need them, but if you want to run a few blind items in your column, go ahead. Check up on the two laundry men who were killed and do something on them—anything else of that nature you can do without being sued. If nothing else, it'll make Clark more nervous."

He smiled. "That I can do—with pleasure."

"And there's only one more thing. If I find Rako, I'll phone you. It'll be your story. Write it that way. Keep my name out of it. As far as you're concerned, you never heard of me."

He looked at me and his eyebrows went up. "What's this—a gag? You don't want any publicity?"

"Not a line," I said.

"Now I've heard everything—after thirty years in this business."

"It's really very simple," I said. "Publicity wouldn't get me any more money than I can get now on a case. And it would make me better known to people I might have to get on my next case. I don't want any rewards except the ones that are signed by the treasurer of the insurance company. I like to make my own trouble. I don't want more made by publicity."

"It makes sense," he said. He put his pencil away. "I'm glad it's a practical reason. After twenty years in Washington, I don't believe there are any other reasons. Want to order lunch?"

"Why not?"

He picked up the menu. "I can recommend the veal in wine."

"I'll try it."

He was right. The veal was good. We both had coffee and brandy and skipped the dessert.

"I'm going to have to run in a minute," he said, glancing at his watch. "I'll have the photograph sent over to your hotel. Which one are you at?"

"The Peraton."

He nodded. "I'll start running some items, and we'll see if we can't make Mr. Clark sweat a little while you're searching. How about letting me show you the town tonight?"

"I'll let you know," I said.

"Good enough." He beckoned the waiter, who brought the check over. He signed it and stood up. "Good luck," he said soberly.

"Thanks."

He turned and left. I finished my coffee slowly, then walked outside. I stepped up to the curb and looked for a taxi. I was still looking when the sedan pulled up abreast of me. Jerry Dell was sitting on the near side and the other fellow was driving. Dell was holding a gun in his lap, but it was pointed at me.

"You want a ride, baby?" he asked.

"Not with you, baby."

"Well, you're getting one. We don't like where you went this morning, and we're all going to sit down and have a nice little talk about it. Lefty, get out and get in the back seat so you can hold a gun on baby. I'll drive."

I glanced around. There were very few people on the street. There was a cop coming toward us, but he was a good block away and taking his time. I looked back into the car. The driver had his door open and was halfway out. Dell was starting to edge over toward the steering wheel.

"You get in the front seat with me, baby," he said.

I shifted my cigarette from my left hand to my right and rested my hand on the open window. Jerry Dell's face was no more than a foot away. I flicked the cigarette directly into it.

At the same time I leaped toward the rear of the car. I heard a curse from Dell, then the low, tense voice of Lefty.

"There's a cop coming." He was sliding back under the wheel. The motor gunned and the car took off.

"Hey there," a voice shouted from behind me. I looked around. It was the cop, who was now advancing at a lumbering run. I waited for him.

"What's going on here?" he demanded as he came up.

"You know as much as I do, officer. Two men wanted me to get into the car with them. I don't know if they were hold-up men or perverts."

"Yeah? Did you get the license number?"

"No. I heard you yell and turned around before I had a chance. Didn't you get it?"

He looked at me with disgust. "All right. Get going." I started to obey, but his voice stopped me. "Just a minute." I turned back to face him. His hand had dropped down to his holster. "Is that a gun you're carrying?"

"Sure," I said.

"Turn around," he said tightly, "and put your hands on top of your head."

I obeyed. "In my right-hand coat pocket you'll find a permit for the gun."

His hand fumbled in my pocket, then came out. There was a moment of silence. "A private dick," he said disgustedly. "All right. Put your hands down and turn around." When I turned, he handed my permit back to me. "Now, what was going on here?"

"I told you all I know. I'm just passing through Washington.

I had lunch in there with a friend of mine and was going back to my hotel when that car pulled up where I was waiting for a taxi. I never saw them before."

"How come you got a Washington permit if you don't work here?"

"Sometimes I do work here."

"When are you leaving?"

"Soon."

He scratched his head. "I ought to run you in anyway," he said. "Okay. On your way."

There was a taxi cruising down the street. I hailed it and went back to the hotel. When I got there, I called the cab company and asked them to send the driver I'd had that morning. About twenty minutes later the desk clerk phoned to say that my taxi was there. I went down and told Irving to take me to the airport. There was no sedan in sight as we pulled away.

"What happened to your escort?" Irving asked.

"They're probably reporting," I said. "They tried to pick me up when I left the restaurant. We had a small argument about it and then a cop came along, so they beat it. I haven't seen them since."

"It'll be lonesome without them," he said with a grin.

When we reached the airport I had him wait. I went inside and started down the line of companies that had flights to San Francisco. The first one was Northwest. There were several pretty girls behind the counter. One of them moved over to meet me as I approached.

"Hello," I said. "Do you have any flights to San Francisco between five-thirty and seven-thirty in the afternoon?"

"Yes, sir. We have one at six-fifteen. Would you like to make a reservation?"

"Not at the moment. Do you know if you've had that schedule for long?"

"I think so, but I wouldn't know."

"Is there anyone here who would know?"

"I don't believe so."

"Where are the old records kept?"

"I imagine at the offices downtown," she said. She looked as if she were about to ask some questions of her own.

"Thank you," I said gravely, and took off. A half hour later I had covered all of the airlines. There were only two that had flights scheduled during the time period I was interested in. One was Northwest and the other was Pan-World, which had a flight at six-thirty.

I had the taxi take me back into the heart of the city. Our first stop was the Northwest office. After talking to three or four people I finally ended up with a vice-president. I showed him my identification, including a card that said I worked for Intercontinental, and told him what I wanted.

"Normally, we don't give out information except to the police," he said, "but in this case I think I can tell you there's no point in looking up the old records."

"Why not?"

"You said seven years ago. Well, we've only had that six-fifteen flight for a little more than two years. Before that we had a five-thirty flight and the next one was at eight."

"Okay, thanks," I said.

I went back to the taxi and we drove on to the Pan-World

building. Again I tracked down a vice-president and made my little speech.

"Well, this is a little unusual," he said. He picked up my identification cards and looked at them. "You work for Intercontinental Insurance?"

"Yes. As an investigator."

"I see. And what does this have to do with one of our flights made seven years ago?"

"I can't tell you the whole case," I said, "but it has to do with a man who disappeared seven years ago. We have reason to believe that the man is still alive, but if we don't find him the courts may soon declare him legally dead, and it will be rather expensive for Intercontinental. I personally think that he took a plane to San Francisco—possibly your six-thirty flight."

"Well, all we'd have would be the passenger list. Do you think you can tell anything from that?"

"I think I might."

"Our policy is that we only give out such information to the police," he said. "I can, however, see your point, but I'll have to get in touch with the home office in New York. They may or may not see it your way."

"How long will that take?" I asked. "I was hoping I could leave Washington tonight."

"I'm afraid we can't do it that quickly," he said with a smile. "Suppose you come back in the morning. I might have an answer by then."

"All right," I said. There was nothing else to say. "I'll see you in the morning."

I went back downstairs and had the cab driver take me to the hotel. As I entered, I saw that Jerry Dell and the other fellow were back on the job.

The photograph from the newspaper was waiting for me at the desk. I took it and went upstairs. It was a good shot of Rako sitting at a table in the hearing room. There was no hat on his head and it was a full-face picture.

After a while I called George Macklin and told him I'd be in town overnight. He told me to meet him for dinner at a place called the Cloisters. I said I would.

I spent the rest of the afternoon taking it easy. Finally I took a shower and changed clothes. I went downstairs and took a cab to the Cloisters. The sedan obediently followed.

George Macklin was waiting for me at a table. He'd been right. It was a good restaurant. The martinis were almost perfect.

I gave him a quick report on the futility of the afternoon, and then we turned the conversation to more interesting things. We had several drinks and then a fine dinner. We were working on the coffee and brandy when he brought us back to business.

"We're about to have company," he said.

I looked around and there was Johnny Clark approaching us. He came up to the table, pulled out a chair, and sat down.

"Hi, Milo," he said. "How are you, Macklin?"

"I was fine," George said.

"Sorry to hear it," Johnny Clark said. He looked at me. "I hear you roughed up one of my boys this morning."

"You heard right," I said. "He put his hand on me. I'm particular about who does that."

"Then, later, you threw a burning cigarette into his face. That wasn't smart, Milo. Jerry's pretty mad."

"That's too bad. But you can tell him he was lucky. The next time he pulls a gun on me, it may be worse. Was that your idea?"

"You misunderstood it. He was just going to bring you to the office so we could have a little chat."

"With a gun in my back?"

"Maybe he was afraid you'd take another punch at him. You shouldn't have thrown that cigarette in his face. Jerry's a tough boy when he's sore."

"I'll try to remember that," I said evenly. "What did you want to talk about?"

"Oh, anything."

"Were you going to tell me where to find Rako?"

"I told you I don't know anything about that."

"So you did. Maybe you were going to tell me why two of your hoods have been following me."

"I told you I don't like cops on my back."

"Or maybe you wanted to tell me about two of your union members who helped Rako vanish and then were killed. Or maybe you wanted to talk about Willie Nemo."

"I don't know what the hell you're talking about," he said angrily. "I just thought we'd have a friendly talk."

"Sorry," I said. "I don't have any time. I expect to take a plane to San Francisco tomorrow."

"Really?" he said. "Have a nice trip." He got up abruptly and walked away.

"What did you say that for?" George Macklin asked. "You don't even know you're going there."

"But I'll bet I'm warm," I said. "He didn't look relieved when he took off. But to hell with him. I thought you were going to show me the town."

"Will do," he said.

We finished our coffee and went pub-crawling. It was almost three in the morning when I made it back to the hotel. I slept until eight and then got up, a little the worse for the night before. But a couple of drinks and some breakfast fixed me up. I got dressed and headed for Pan-World.

The vice-president was waiting for me when I was shown into his office. "You're in luck, March," he said. "The New York office said to give you the information. It seems we have quite a bit of insurance with your company."

"That always helps," I said.

"We had a flight to San Francisco at six-thirty on May 6th seven years ago. I have the passenger list right here, but I don't think it's going to tell you much. You want me to read the names to you?"

"I don't think that would help," I said. "Was the flight completely booked?"

"Yes."

"Any last-minute tickets sold?"

"As a matter of fact there was one—by accident. The flight was all reserved, but one passenger didn't show, and that seat was given to a stand-by passenger who was waiting at the counter. It happens quite often."

"Sure," I said. "What about the one that didn't show? When was his reservation made?"

"About one-thirty in the afternoon—by phone. A Mr. Joseph

Smith. He didn't cancel or anything. We probably held the ticket until shortly after six, although I have no record on that, and then turned it over to a man who had been waiting at the terminal."

"What was his name?"

"R. Thomas."

"Smith and Thomas," I said. "Two good old American names. Well, thanks."

I left before he could ask any questions. On the way out I stopped and made a reservation on the next plane to San Francisco.

I took a cab back to the hotel, packed, and checked out. I went to the airport and checked my bag. There was just time to get a newspaper, some cigarettes, and a quick drink. Then I boarded the plane.

Shortly before the plane took off, a last-minute passenger hurried in and took a seat behind me. It was Jerry Dell.

EIGHT

It was still early evening when the plane came down in San Francisco. I took a taxi to the Imperial Hotel and checked in. Jerry Dell was approaching the desk as I went upstairs. I unpacked my things when I got to the room and put them away. Then I slept until evening. I went downstairs and ordered a martini. As I nursed it, I thought about the case.

Now that I was in San Francisco, what the hell was I going to do? Where did you start to pick up a trail that was seven years old? The only thing I could think of was my one contact, Pete Moretti. He'd been in the rackets in New York and he was in trouble with the boys who ran things. I'd bumped into the situation while I was working on a case involving some of the hoods who were after him. I'd saved his life. I remembered hearing that he'd come to San Francisco and was running a club. I pulled out my address book and thumbed through it. Sure enough, it was there. The Club Moretti on Broadway.

I looked around the room to see if Jerry Dell was waiting as usual. I didn't see him, but I did see somebody else I wasn't expecting. Nick Potti was sitting in a booth along the wall.

I finished my martini and walked over. "It looks like I'm hitting the jackpot," I said. "I draw you and Jerry Dell both. I'm flattered."

"I don't know what you're talking about," he said. "I'm here on business."

"I know—and I'm it. Where's your twin?"

"Jerry? I guess he's upstairs. I told you. We're both here on union business."

"So am I. Rako." I looked up and saw Dell approaching from the lobby. "Here he is now. I'm glad he made it. I was just ready to leave and I wouldn't want to lose either one of you boys. You might get a lesson in how to enjoy yourself in San Francisco." I turned and left the bar.

The doorman got a taxi for me. As it pulled away, I looked back and saw Jerry Dell and Nick Potti getting into another cab. I turned back and told my driver where I wanted to go.

I went to the Four Seas on Grant Avenue. I had another drink, then the barbecued Mongolian lamb. It was one of the best meals I'd had in a long time, and it was made even more enjoyable by watching Dell and Potti, who had followed me in, struggling over the menu. It was mostly Northern Chinese food and therefore completely strange to the person who is familiar with the average Cantonese restaurant.

I lingered over the tea and finally left. Then I took my two faithful followers on a short tour of San Francisco, mostly to throw them off about the visit I wanted to make. I made stops at the hungry i, the Purple Onion, the Black Hawk, and finally the Buena Vista, where I had some Irish coffee. It was about ten o'clock when I left there and went to the Club Moretti.

There was a small jazz combo playing when I entered. I got a table near them. Dell and Potti came in and took a table not far from where I sat. I wondered if they knew Pete Moretti.

I had a drink and when the waiter came over to see if I wanted another one, I told him I wanted to see the headwaiter. I'd tipped him well when I first came in, so he responded quickly.

"Is there anything wrong, sir?" the headwaiter asked.

"No," I said. "Is Pete Moretti in?"

"I don't know, sir," he said evasively. "Perhaps I can help you."

"Tell Pete that Milo March is out here and wants to talk to him. But I don't want to be obvious about it. I'd like to handle it so that no one knows I'm going to see him. I'll do whatever he suggests."

"I'll see, sir," he said, and slipped away.

I listened to the combo and waited. They were good. They finished one number and were starting on another when I saw my waiter coming. He was carrying a fresh drink for me.

"Sorry, sir," he said, his voice low as he picked up my empty glass. "I have instructions to spill this drink on you and to tell you to make a scene when it happens."

"All right," I said. I got out a cigarette and started to light it.

He set the drink in front of me and started to turn away. As he did, his tray hit the glass. It and the emptied glass both landed in my lap. I leaped to my feet.

"What the hell's the matter with you?" I said loudly. "Drunk or something? Look at my suit."

"I'm sorry, sir," he said. He was mopping at my pants with a napkin.

"To hell with being sorry. What about my suit?"

The waiter glanced around nervously as though he were

worried about the other customers witnessing this scene. He gave up trying to dry off my suit and straightened up.

"If you'll just follow me, sir, everything will be taken care of."

"It had better be," I said as I followed him.

It was hard to keep from smiling as we went past the table where Dell and Potti sat. I could see they weren't sure whether this was on the level or not. In the meantime the waiter turned and headed toward the rear of the room. We went all the way to the back, then turned into a little corridor. There were several doors opening off it. We stopped at the first one.

"In there, sir," he said.

"Thanks," I told him.

I opened the door and stepped inside. Pete Moretti was sitting behind a desk covered with papers. He was a big man with dark hair, now beginning to thin. Otherwise he looked about the same as the last time I'd seen him.

He looked up as I closed the door and a smile spread over his face. "Milo," he said. "It's good to see you. How'd you like the service?"

"Great," I said, looking down at my wet trousers, "but couldn't you have figured out a way that wouldn't look so much like a part of an old Buster Keaton movie?"

He chuckled. "You wanted action, so I gave it to you. How the hell are you, anyway?"

"Pretty good."

I walked over to the desk and shook hands with him. I dropped into the chair beside his desk and got out a cigarette to replace the one I'd just started to light when the drink went into my lap.

He opened a drawer of the desk and pulled out a glass and a bottle of V.O. He poured a drink and pushed it over. "To replace the one you lost," he said. "The waiter said that's what you were drinking. In town on business or pleasure?"

"Business."

"Somebody on your tail?"

I nodded. "Two fellows you might know and they might know you. That's why I didn't want to be obvious about coming back. They're sitting out there now."

"Who?"

"Jerry Dell and Nick Potti."

His face became serious. "I used to know Dell and I've heard of Potti. Guns—and good ones. Do they mean business?"

"Not yet, but they may before long."

"You want them taken off your back?"

I shook my head. "But I do want a favor from you, if it's possible."

"I owe you a favor," he said quietly.

"Do you still have contacts?"

"I have a few. What is it, Milo?"

"Do you remember the name Thomas Rako?"

He frowned. "Sure. I never knew him. He was a gun, too. Not as good as these two. He made a showing before a Washington hearing, then vanished. My guess was that somebody let a contract on him."

"I don't think so," I said. "I think he's still alive and hiding out somewhere. I'm trying to find him for an insurance company. The two boys outside don't want me to find him. They both work for Johnny Clark. So did Rako."

"You think he's out here?"

"I doubt it. But I think he came here from Washington and then went on somewhere else. He'd need a lot of help to vanish so completely. He had it in Washington. He could get it almost anywhere through Clark's union, but he may have had some contacts of his own out here. He was here when he was a kid and got his first conviction here. But direct help I'm sure was dangerous for everybody."

"How?"

"Two union members helped him in Washington and they were both dead within a week. They were probably killed by a small-time hood, who also turned up dead."

"Covering up the trail, huh? I don't get it. Rako wasn't that big a man. Why should anybody go to so much trouble for him?"

"I think he had something on Clark and still has."

He nodded. "What do you want, Milo?"

"I'm pretty sure that Rako came here the evening of May 6th seven years ago. From there on, I'm riding blind. I'd like to know where he went from here."

"I'll see what I can do. Where're you staying?"

"The Imperial."

"Stay around there tomorrow and I'll call you."

"Thanks, Pete."

He waved his hand. "You earned it years ago. I'll be talking to you sometime tomorrow."

I left the office and went back the way I'd come. Dell and Potti were still at their table, looking nervous, until they caught sight of me. Then they relaxed. I sat down at my table and the waiter came over.

"Everything all right, sir?" he asked with a little smile.

"Everything is fine. Bring me a double V.O. Not to be spilled."

"Yes, sir."

He returned with my drink and I settled back to enjoy the combo. They played strictly Chicago-style jazz and it was good to hear again. Later there was a singer, a girl who reminded me of Pearl Bailey. Finally, about twelve o'clock, I decided I'd had enough. I paid my check and gave the waiter a little extra on the tip. I walked over to the table where Jerry Dell and Nick Potti were paying their check.

"Relax, boys," I said. "I'm just going back to the hotel, so both of you will be able to turn in and get your beauty sleep. Especially you, Jerry, baby."

They both glared at me as I left.

I went out and got a taxi back to the hotel. I picked up a newspaper and some cigarettes and went to my room, where I got undressed, turned on the TV set to the late movie, and got into bed. I browsed through the paper and then watched the movie until I fell asleep—just before Clark Gable was going to kiss the broad.

I slept until nine-thirty the next morning. Then I showered and shaved, and got back into bed before calling room service. I had ham and eggs and a big pot of coffee. I got dressed and faced the fact that I might have to stay in the room for several hours. Next I called the operator and told her I was going to the lobby for a minute and if a call came for me to hold it until I got back.

I went downstairs and looked around to see if either of my tails was on watch. One was—Jerry Dell. I bought some magazines and went back upstairs.

At one o'clock I had two martinis and a hot turkey sandwich sent up. Then I went back to reading. Finally, at four o'clock, the phone rang. I picked it up and said hello.

"Milo, this is Pete," he said. "I've got something for you. Come over to the club. It's closed, but Mario will be watching for you and let you in. Only lose your two boys. How well do you know San Francisco?"

"Not too well. I've been here a couple of times. Mostly I know the clubs and the restaurants."

"All right. Go to Cost Plus on Taylor Street, down close to Fisherman's Wharf. It's a split-level bargain basement store with very good stuff. It also has more than one exit. You should be able to lose them there."

"Okay," I said. "I'll be at the club as soon as I can."

I hung up, put on my tie and coat, and was ready. I went downstairs. Dell and Potti were both in the lobby looking as if they were tired of waiting. They straightened up in their chairs as I went by.

I got a cab and told the driver to take me to Cost Plus on Taylor Street. He nodded and took off. I looked back and saw them getting into a taxi.

We reached the store and the driver pulled into the curb. I leaned forward.

"Keep the flag down," I said. I got out enough money to cover the amount on the meter and handed it to him.

Then I added a five-dollar bill. "I want something for it," I said.

"What?" he asked.

"Leave the flag down and wait for ten minutes. Then you can throw the flag up and take off with the five bucks."

"Somebody following you?"

"That's right. But he won't bother you. The minute you leave he'll come storming into the store. Okay?"

"Okay," he said stolidly.

I got out of the cab noticing that their cab was about forty feet back and waiting. I nodded to the driver and went into the store. I started through it and then stopped at a counter. I bought an Italian wine liter for a dollar.

"Is there another way out of the store," I asked the salesgirl, "than the Taylor Street entrance?"

"Yes, sir," she said. "That way." She pointed.

I followed her directions and soon found myself out on another street. I didn't bother to see what street it was. I was in luck. A passenger was just getting out of a taxi. I climbed in and told the driver to go to Broadway.

I had checked several times, and when we reached Broadway I was sure we weren't being followed. Then I told the driver I wanted the Club Moretti.

"It ain't open," he said.

"I know," I told him. "I only like closed nightclubs, so take me there anyway."

He grunted and continued to drive. I kept checking the rear

window, but there was nobody following us. It was still that way when we reached the club, I paid him and went to the front door. It was immediately opened by a man I recognized as the headwaiter of the night before.

"The boss is in the office," he said.

I walked back through the empty club. There's nothing more dismal-looking than a nightclub when the chairs are all stacked on the tables and there's nobody around. I went straight through the corridor to the first door. This time I knocked on it.

"Come in," his voice said.

I opened the door and went in. Pete Moretti was busy at his desk, but he leaned back and smiled when he saw me.

"You know," he said, "I never guessed there so much paper-work in this racket or I might've stayed out of it."

"From the looks of the club last night, you must be doing all right."

"I can't complain. And I got a couple of other things going for me. Sit down, Milo. Drink?"

"Sure," I said, taking a chair.

He poured a drink and handed it to me. "I got something for you, not much, but it's all I could dig up. It wasn't easy at that. You ever hear of Manny Roberts?"

"Sure. The bookie king of the East Coast."

He nodded. "He's in New York and he's got at least a piece of the action around there. It ain't exactly like the newspapers say. There's other fellows in, say, Philadelphia, but Manny's got New York City and up the river about halfway to Albany. It ain't a bad territory."

"I guess not," I said with a smile.

"Well, that's where your Rako went. He was sent there by a fellow I know here. All he did was pass Rako along to Roberts. He doesn't know what happened to him after that."

"This fellow tied in with Johnny Clark?"

"No. He has his own things going for him. But Rako must've come pretty well recommended or he wouldn't have gotten in even to see this guy."

"Well, thanks, Pete."

"Nothing to it. I told you it wasn't much, but at least it pinpoints him for you."

"Some pinpoint—New York City and halfway to Albany. But it does point me in the right direction. And I appreciate it, Pete."

"Just forget where you learned it." He pushed a button on his desk. "And watch your step with Dell and Potti. They're both bad boys to tangle with."

"I'll watch it."

The door opened and the headwaiter looked in. "Check the back door, Mario,"

Pete Moretti said. "If it's clear, let my friend out that way." He looked at me. "There's a taxi out there that's been waiting since I called you. But don't take it straight to the hotel. There are some people who know that the driver works for me."

I stood up and shook hands with him. "Thanks again, Pete. I'll be seeing you."

"I'll be here. I'm even beginning to like this quiet life."

I followed the headwaiter to the back door. He opened it and looked out. "Everything's clear," he said.

"Thanks, Mario."

I stepped out and saw the taxi parked there. I went over and climbed in. I told him to take me to a bar I remembered that was not far off Broadway near Chinatown. It took only a few minutes to get there. I paid him off and added a big tip because he'd waited for me. I went in and sat at the bar. It was getting close to cocktail time and there were several other people already there.

I took my drink slowly, watching the place fill up. It was mostly a business crowd, men and women both. Finally I ordered a second drink and sipped it. I was in no hurry, and the longer I was lost the more it would worry Dell and Potti.

I'd been there about an hour by the time I finished my second drink, so I paid the check and left, taking a taxi back to the hotel. I stopped at the desk.

"I'd like to get a plane to New York tonight or the first thing in the morning. Will you take care of it for me?"

"Certainly, sir. There's a jet leaving here at midnight that will get you in early in the morning, New York time. Shall I try that one first?"

"Fine. The name's Milo March. I'll be in my room. Oh, by the way, do you know if Mr. Dell and Mr. Potti have returned to the hotel?"

"Oh, yes, they returned some time ago. As a matter of fact Mr. Dell checked out about an hour ago."

That caught me off base. "Checked out?"

"Yes. I believe he said something about a sudden appointment in New York. Anyway, we were able to get him on a plane almost at once."

"And Mr. Potti?"

"I believe he's in the bar, sir."

"All right. Let me know about the reservation."

I turned and went to the elevators. Upstairs, I sat down to wait. So Jerry Dell had gone ahead to New York. I'd have only one of them on my tail, but I'd have the other one step ahead of me. I didn't like that, even though it meant that the trail was getting warmer.

The phone rang. It was the clerk. "I have you booked on the midnight flight, Mr. March. You can pick up your ticket here."

"Thanks. I'll be down in a few minutes."

I hung up and started packing. When I'd finished, I went downstairs. I stopped at the desk and paid my bill and picked up the airplane ticket.

"I left my luggage in the room," I said. "Have a boy pick it up and bring it down here. I'm going to have dinner in the hotel dining room and I'll leave later."

"All right, Mr. March."

I went into the bar. Nick Potti was there, sitting at the bar this time. I went over and took the next stool. I ordered a martini.

Nick looked at me coldly. "Think you're pretty smart, don't you?"

"I can't imagine what you mean, Nick," I said.

"Shaking us at that crummy store this afternoon."

"Oh, that. You know how it is, Nick. A man wants a little privacy once in a while. Where's your little playmate?"

"He had to leave … on business."

"That's what I heard. I guess he chickened out. Sure you can handle the job by yourself?"

"I can handle it."

"That's what I like in a man—self-confidence. How did Johnny Clark feel when you called to tell him you'd lost me?"

He looked at me. "I don't like you, March. It's going to be a real pleasure if you step out of line."

"It's a funny world. Johnny Clark likes me and you don't like me, but you both want the same thing to happen to me." I glanced at my watch.

"What's your hurry?" he said. "You're not going anyplace until the midnight plane."

"You've been snooping again, Nick."

He smiled, but there was no humor in it. "I saw you come in. I thought you did a lot of talking to the clerk. So I went out and hung around the desk. I heard him make the reservation for you and then call you."

"And I suppose you now have a reservation on the same plane?"

"That's right."

"That's good. I don't know what I'd do without one of you around. I'm going to miss you when you're gone."

"What does that crack mean?"

"I thought it was clear enough," I said. I glanced at my watch again. "I'm going to have some dinner. And don't bother joining me. I want to be able to keep it down." I left money on the bar for the bartender and walked out.

I had a long, leisurely dinner. I followed it with two cups of coffee and then decided I might as well kill the rest of the time at the airport. I went out and ransomed my luggage from the bellhop. He carried it out to the curb and the doorman whistled for a cab.

I saw Nick Potti hurrying out of the hotel with his luggage. It amused me. I got into the taxi and told the driver where I wanted to go. I didn't bother looking back this time.

When I reached the airport I checked my suitcase at the counter and went into the cocktail lounge. Nick Potti came in shortly afterward. He didn't bother coming near me but took a table close to the door.

Finally it was flight time. I went aboard and as soon as the plane was in the air I went to sleep. I slept all the way back to New York.

It was cheerful daylight when I left the plane in New York. I waited at the luggage counter and reclaimed my baggage. Then I waited at one side until Nick had his.

"I thought I'd save you some worry," I told him. "I'm going to go to my apartment on Perry Street and get some more sleep. You can stand out on the street and watch if you like."

He made a suggestion about what I could do. It was both rude and impossible, so I didn't answer. I went out and got a cab and gave the driver my address.

When I finally let myself into my apartment it was almost nine o'clock. I made myself a cup of instant coffee and poured a little brandy into it. Then I set the alarm for eleven o'clock and went back to sleep.

When I awakened, I put on a pot of coffee and showered while it was percolating. I had a cup and decided it was time I got to work. I picked up the phone and dialed the number of police headquarters. I asked for Lieutenant Rockland.

"Johnny," I said when he answered, "this is Milo."

"I thought you were out of town."

"I was. I just got in this morning."

"What do you want this time?" he asked. "You never call unless you want something."

"Do you know Manny Roberts?"

"Do I know who's buried in Grant's Tomb? I'm a cop. Remember?"

"Suppose he wanted to help a guy disappear. What do you think he'd do?"

"If I know Manny, he'd have the guy shot, put in a bale of scrap metal, and sold to a smelter."

"No, this would be a man who had to be kept alive."

"What are you working on, Milo?"

"Thomas Rako. The Carrier Workers union guy who disappeared seven years ago right after making an appearance before a Congressional committee."

"You think he's still alive?"

"I'm pretty sure he is. He was sent to Manny Roberts for help in his vanishing act. I imagine that he got it because I'm told he came highly recommended."

"By whom?"

"Some man on the West Coast. I don't know his name. But I think you can also bet that Johnny Clark had a hand in it all the way. Where do you think Roberts would hide Rako that would be good for the last seven years?"

"Why should they bother hiding him? I don't get that part of it. Are they suddenly getting ethical or something?"

"I think he has something on Clark and that's been his insurance."

"Interesting. Well, they could have kept him here in the

city. It's a big place. But I doubt if they'd do that. New Yorkers are too hip about things, and there would be too many people who might spot him one day. If what you say is true, I guess they wouldn't send him out of the country. Clark would want him where he could keep a check on him. Did he have any money?"

"I think he had seventy-five thousand that Clark gave him, and I'm sure he could get more."

"Then why not stick him in some hick town? He could buy a little hardware store, keep his nose clean, and probably look like a native by now."

"I had something like that in mind," I said. "But they'd probably keep him within Manny Roberts's territory."

He was silent for a minute. "Well, Roberts has most of the bookies from here to halfway to Albany, but his out-of-town operation has its headquarters in Orange County—in Newburgh. We raided a few places in the city here a few months ago and got the leads to some of his places up there. We passed them along to the State Police, who closed up seven or eight of his places, but that was only a drop in the bucket. You might try up there."

"I might as well start there as anywhere," I agreed with a sigh. "It's like looking for a needle in a haystack, only the needle may look like a thimble now. Seven years and money can make a lot of changes in a man."

"Well, you can always take up sewing," he said cheerfully. "Anything else I can do for you?"

"No, but maybe I can do something for you. Know Jerry Dell?"

"I used to know him when he worked around here," he said. His voice sounded peculiar. "Why do you ask?"

"He's in New York."

"Is that so?" he asked sarcastically. "Do you mean to tell me that he came in last night on a flight from San Francisco?"

"You know, huh? How'd you stumble onto that so fast?"

"Look who's talking about stumbling when you always have to call me for help. One of my men was out at the airport last night on another assignment that didn't work out. He spotted Dell and followed him to a hotel. Dell spells trouble, so I put a stakeout on the hotel."

"That's a break," I said. "Who'd he see in New York?"

"Nobody, unless it was somebody who sneaked into the hotel. He never left it until this morning, when he went to Forty-first Street and took a bus out of the city."

"A bus? Where to?"

"How the hell do I know? As soon as my man saw he was leaving the city, he came back here. We're only worried when he's in the city."

"It wouldn't have hurt to get at least a general idea of where he was headed."

"I can tell you that," he said cheerfully. "He went downstairs and he didn't take a long-distance bus. So that means that he took a bus headed for upstate."

"Well, that's something," I admitted. "That makes Orange County look even better than it did when you mentioned it before."

"I'm glad that it pleases you," he said. His voice was heavy with sarcasm. "The department of police exists only to serve the public."

"It's good to learn that you know your place," I said. "Thanks, Johnny." I hung up.

I went into my kitchenette and made myself some bacon and eggs and a couple of slices of toast. Then I had another cup of coffee.

I rummaged through the apartment and found a New York map. It took me a few minutes, but I finally located Newburgh. I decided I wouldn't go directly there. Instead, I'd fix myself somewhere near it. I picked on a town called Cornwall-on-Hudson, which was about five miles from Newburgh. I noted that it was right off Route 9-W and put the map away.

I thought of calling Martin Raymond but decided against it. I didn't have enough to report, and I wasn't that fond of conversing with him. I unpacked my suitcase and put fresh clothes in it. Then I dressed and went downstairs.

He was waiting across the street in a taxi. I walked up to Fourth Street and then down to Sheridan Square, with Potti's taxi creeping along behind me until I reached Fourth and then sprinting to Seventh Avenue where it could turn down to meet me. I got a taxi at Fourth and Seventh and told the driver where to take me. It was a car rental place—not the one that puts you in the driver's seat,* but then I always liked to climb in myself. I went in and rented a new Mercury sedan. When I drove out in it, Nick Potti and his taxi were still waiting. The taxi followed as I headed west. I smiled to myself. He was going to have a nice cab fare by the time he got through with me.

---

* "Let Hertz put you in the driver's seat" was a familiar commercial jingle in the mid-1960s.

I hit the West Side highway and drove up to the George Washington Bridge. When I reached the end of the bridge, I turned right onto the Palisades parkway. The taxi was still on my tail. I probably could've lost him once I was on the parkway, but I didn't even try.

An hour and ten minutes and sixty miles later, I was getting close to Bear Mountain, and when I reached the bottom there was a sign indicating the exit for Cornwall. I turned off into it and the taxi dutifully followed. I took another right, and two minutes later I was in the middle of a sleepy little village. You could see the whole length of the main street. There were only two bars on the street. I pulled down to the second one, mostly because it was called the B&B, which I figured meant broads and booze. I parked and went inside without looking at the taxi.

It was a typical small-town bar. There was a bowling machine, a jukebox, a cigarette machine, and the bar. There was a room in the back, but it was dark and empty. Three men sat at the bar—all with beers in front of them. I sat at the end of the bar, where I could see through the window. The bartender came over. He was a short, heavyset young fellow who looked Irish.

"V.O. on the rocks," I said. "Make it a double. Not too much ice. I don't want to go skating."

He smiled and went away to come back with a glass and one ice cube. He poured out the two shots and left the bottle. I put two bills on the bar and he gave me eighty cents in change— one of the advantages of drinking in a small town.

"A quiet town," I said.

"You can say that again," he said. "You from the city?"

I nodded. "Thought I'd try a little vacation up here for a few days. You know, peace and quiet."

"You'll find that. Maybe even a piece, if you're looking."

"I'm always looking. You don't sound like a native son."

"I came up from the city eight years ago," he said, "and took over this place. Believe me, if I could find a buyer, I'd go back. You wouldn't like to buy a good bar, would you?"

"Not me. I have too many bars all over the country I have to support. It wouldn't be fair." He laughed and I waited until he had enjoyed it. "Is there a decent motel around here where I can stay?"

"You're driving?"

I nodded.

"Up that street there," he said, "about a mile, just past 9-W. Nice rooms. TV. And they don't look too closely if you want a friend to visit you."

"Sounds good," I said. And noticed, by looking through the window, that Nick Potti had been having a long talk with the taxi driver. He must have lost his argument, because he'd just paid off the driver and climbed out. "What does somebody do around here if he wants a taxi?"

"Phone. I thought you said you were driving."

"I am. I was just curious." I finished my drink. "I guess I'll go along and register in the motel. I'll be around later."

"Okay," he said. He smiled and held out his hand. "I'm Eddie Sales."

"Milo March," I said as we shook hands. "Tell me, is there a slightly roundabout way for me to reach that motel without going straight up that street?"

His expression became more alert. "The guy who just got out of the New York City cab?" he asked. He kept his voice low so that the men at the bar couldn't hear him.

"That's about the size of it," I said. "I'd rather he wasn't sure which direction I was taking."

"Go back up the street," he said, "take the second right. It runs at a diagonal. That'll bring you back into the main street. Then make a left and go straight ahead until you hit the motel."

"Thanks," I said. "I'll see you later." I got up and walked out.

Nick Potti was in a public phone booth on the sidewalk. I enjoyed the expression on his face as I got in the car, made a U-turn, and sped away. I turned right at the second street, then left at the next one. I went over a bridge crossing a highway that must've been 9-W, and shortly after that I saw the motel. I pulled in and registered. I was shown to my cabin and put the car beside it, trying to park it an angle so that the license plate wouldn't show from the road. I went inside. It was a nice room.

I realized that I was tired. I'd had a few hours' sleep on the plane and then less than two hours in my apartment. I took off my coat and tie and stretched out on the bed. I went to sleep almost immediately.

It was six o'clock when I awakened. I felt a little better. I got up and washed my face. I put on my tie and coat and went out. I drove back the way I had come. This time I noticed that there were signs all along the street commemorating something that had happened there during the Revolution. I was to learn later that the whole area was full of historic monuments, many of them still walking the streets.

There was no sign that I was being followed, the first time in the last four days. Not that it mattered much. If Rako was in this neighborhood, Dell was probably already here, and they'd concentrate on Rako to make sure that I didn't get too near.

I pulled in beside the B&B and parked, then went inside. This time the bar was busy. I finally found a seat at one end. Eddie Sales saw me and came over with the bottle of V.O. and a glass with ice in it.

"A double?" he asked.

I nodded and he poured it. "Get settled?" he asked.

"Yes. It seems fine."

"Don't go away," he said. "I have something to tell you, but I have to fill up some empty glasses."

He went to work drawing beers and pouring drinks. I sipped my drink and listened to the talk. The television set was on, but I don't think anybody was watching it. They were all talking, most of them about other people. From the little I heard, I decided that if I spent a week there, I'd know all about the sex lives of the entire village. There were a few women at the bar, most of whom had seen better years, but they had the most to contribute to the local folklore.

Eddie Sales got everyone satisfied and came back. He rested his face on one fist; it seemed that was done to make it harder for the man on the next stool to hear.

"What is this?" I asked. "Peyton Place?"

He smiled. "Not far from it. Your friend came in after you left today."

"My friend?"

"Yeah. The guy who got out of the New York City cab while you were here. He wanted to ask some questions about you."

NINE

Somebody wanted a beer and Eddie went off to serve it. He rang up the fifteen cents and came back.

"He wanted to know where you went. I told him you asked the way to Route 32.

You reach it by the way you started, but without making the turn off you made." He seemed very pleased with himself.

"Thanks," I said. "He'll be back. The next time, you can tell him where I am. It's not important and he's a tough boy. I wouldn't want you to get involved."

"I've always got this," he said, showing me a short baseball bat he brought up from under the bar.

"This one doesn't play that way. He uses a gun."

"Is that why you're carrying one?" he asked.

I was surprised. The average person can't spot a gun in a shoulder holster. "What did you say you did in New York City?"

"The same thing I'm doing now. You get so you can spot them. I guess they're handy on a vacation."

"Sure," I said easily. "Especially in the country. There's always wild game. Where's a good place for me to eat?"

"There's a lot of places around here—good ones. You want something near or you feel like driving a few miles?"

"Something near, I guess."

"Go down to the lower village. There's a hotel and restaurant on the left about a half mile from here. It's not cheap, but the food is good."

"Okay," I said. I finished my drink. "I'll see you later." He nodded and went back to work as I left. I drove down the street and easily found the hotel. There was a parking lot in the rear. I put the Mercury there and went in.

The first person I saw as I was being led to a table was Nick Potti. He was sitting at a table all alone and scowling. His face brightened somewhat at the sight of me. I ordered a dry martini, and after I'd had a couple of sips I got up and went over to Nick's table.

"Enjoying yourself, Nick?" I asked.

"What the hell are you doing in this hick town?" he asked. "It's enough to drive a guy nuts."

"It's a pleasant little rural retreat," I said. "All you have to do is relax and enjoy it."

He said his favorite four-letter word.

"Besides," I said, "you should find plenty of friends around. Jerry Dell must be somewhere near here, and I understand that Manny Roberts has a lot of boys around, too. And where you find the boys, there must be some broads."

"You can have all the hick towns in the world. I don't like them."

"Well, you might as well make the best of it, Nick," I said. "We're liable to be here for a few days. Incidentally, if you don't feel like it, you don't have to follow me when I leave after dinner. I'm staying at the George Washington Motel on Cornwall Street. You can find it with no trouble at all."

"Thanks for nothing," he said.

I went back to my table, finished my martini, and ordered dinner.

Eddie Sales had been right. It was good food. After I finished, I went out to the parking lot. As I got into the car I saw that Nick had smartened up. He'd either rented or borrowed a car.

I drove up the street and stopped at a liquor store. I picked up a bottle of V.O. for the motel, then went on to the B&B. There was another man behind the bar this time, but Eddie Sales was out front mixing with the customers. He came over when I sat down and bought me a drink.

Nick Potti came in and went down to the other end of the bar.

"That's him," Eddie Sales said.

"That's him," I agreed. "His name is Nick Potti and he's from Cleveland, Ohio. He's a big man in the gun business. He usually does it only for money, but he's short-tempered and I wouldn't push him if I were you."

"You're exaggerating?" he guessed.

I shook my head. "Not a bit. And there's another one around. A tall, slim guy with straw-colored hair. Calls everybody baby. Maybe you've seen him."

"He hasn't been in here. What do they want up here?"

"Me. But not right at the moment, so you don't have to worry about your place being shot up."

"You a cop?" he asked.

I thought about it a minute before I answered. I was going to need somebody who could answer some questions for me, and maybe Eddie Sales was the answer. He wasn't a native and he probably wasn't part of Manny Roberts's operation. Anyway, I'd been taking chances since I'd started the case.

"No," I said. "Tell me, what do I do around here if I want to put a few bucks on a horse?"

"Most booking goes through Newburgh, but there's a guy who comes in here every day about noon and picks up any bets. Numbers money, too. He stops at all the bars around."

"What do you get out of it?" I asked bluntly.

"Nothing. A customer leaves a note and some money for another customer who picks it up. Me, I don't know what it's all about. But if I didn't do it, those customers would go somewhere else."

"Okay," I said. "I told you I wasn't a cop. It's true. But I work for an insurance company and I have a permit to carry this gun. I'm looking for a man. My friend over there doesn't want me to find him. It's as simple as that."

"Who's he work for?"

"The Carrier Workers Union of America."

He whistled under his breath. "I wouldn't say too much about that around here. The place is full of members, and they swear by Clark."

"I wasn't intending to," I said. "How long did you say you've been here?"

"Eight years, and everybody still acts as if I were a foreigner—the city slicker."

"Many new people move into this section?"

"Usually it's the other way around. A lot of business firms have left here in the last few years. Taxes are too high, and they get no help from the Chamber of Commerce. That's one of the reasons I'd sell if I could. I cash more and more unemployment checks each year."

"How many people do you know who moved here since you came?"

"Not too many, but then I wouldn't know them unless they run other bars or are customers here. I can think of four bar-and-restaurant owners. One's up the street. Another one's over on Route 32, and the other two are on the other side of the thruway. Then there's an Air Force captain who's stationed at Stewart, and there's a writer out in Mountainville. That's about it."

"Tomorrow I'll ask you to look at a photograph." I looked around. "What do you do here for amusement?"

"You're looking at it," he said. He smiled. "Or you meet somebody's wife at a motel the other side of Newburgh."

"I gathered that was a popular sport around here," I said, "from what I heard the customers saying when I was here earlier."

"They're all gabby bitches, aren't they?" he said. "They all have one motto. If you can't say something bitchy about somebody, don't say anything."

"Sounds like a good all-American small town," I said. "Well, I think I'll go turn in. See you tomorrow."

"Okay," he said. "Take it easy."

I slid off the stool and left. As I closed the door I saw Nick Potti gulp down his drink and start after me. There was a store open up the street. I stopped there and picked up a local newspaper and a paperback book. Then I drove straight to the motel and went into my bungalow. I stripped off my clothes, turned on the TV, poured myself a drink, and got into bed with the newspaper.

There wasn't much in it. Newburgh was still fighting the battle of what they called all the bums on welfare, even though they hadn't been able to find more than one man on it who was able to work. They paid a little attention to national news, but not much. I finally gave up and watched television while I had a couple of drinks. Then I went to sleep.

I was up early the next morning and left the motel immediately. Nick must've thought I'd sleep later, for he wasn't in sight. I found a place in the village where I could get some breakfast, then looked up an address in the phone book and drove over to Route 9-W. I headed toward Newburgh and kept going until I came to the State Police barracks. I drove in and parked.

Inside, I faced a stiff-backed young sergeant. "I'd like to see the officer who's in charge," I said.

"That's Lieutenant Pilus," he said. He looked me over carefully. "Do you have a permit for that gun you're carrying?"

"Sure," I said. I fished it out of my pocket and handed it to him.

He looked it over and glanced at me to see if I looked like the photograph. Finally he handed it back to me. "A private detective," he said in about the same tone some people mention cockroaches. "What do you want?"

"I'll discuss it with the Lieutenant," I told him.

He didn't like that, but there wasn't too much he could do about it. He picked up the phone. "There's a private detective from New York City who wants to see you. He won't say what it's about. He's carrying a gun just like a real cop." He listened, then hung up. "The first door on the right."

"You left one thing out, sonny," I said. "I can also use the gun like a real cop." I walked past him and back to the first door. The Lieutenant was seated at a desk. He was a tall, lean man with that starched look that all state cops seem to have.

"You're the private detective?" he asked.

"That's what it says on my license," I said. "The name is Milo March. I'm an insurance investigator." I took out my identification and showed it to him.

He glanced at it briefly. "Is that why you carry a gun?"

"Cops aren't the only people who don't like insurance investigators," I said. "I have a perverse desire to stay alive. I'm bonded and the whole thing is legal, so don't give me any police lectures. If I want to hear any more of them, I'll go to the Academy."

He didn't like that. "I'm not very fond of people carrying guns in my district," he said.

"It's not your district," I pointed out. "You're here to protect the people who live in the district. Now, I'd like a little cooperation. You can either give it or not—and to hell with it."

"Well, you're frank at least," he said with a faint smile. "What do you want?"

"I'm looking for a man. I think he may be in this area and has been for almost seven years. I have a photograph of him taken seven years ago. I wanted to find out if you know anyone who looks like the photo."

"Let's see it."

I took out the photograph of Rako and put it on the desk. He studied it for a minute. "He looks faintly familiar," he said finally, "but I can't place it. Is he on a wanted list?"

"He was. He was a witness before a Congressional committee seven years ago—a hearing on the Carrier Workers union. He disappeared the night of the first hearing."

"That must be why his face is familiar," he said. "Why are you looking for him now?"

"In another month he will be declared legally dead. It'll cost the company a lot of money. So they're interested."

"Naturally. What makes you think he's around here?"

"It's my idea, and I think I'm right."

"I suppose the FBI and various police organizations haven't been looking for him?"

"They have been."

"You think you can find him when they can't?"

"It won't be the first time I've done something they couldn't."

"And you need the gun to take him back? Or do you just wear it to feel big?"

"I wear it so that cops will have something to talk about when they meet me," I said evenly. "Would you like to go into it a little deeper and maybe even discuss the fancy-pants uniform that you wear?"

His face got a little darker. "Leave the photograph," he said curtly, "and your address. If any of my men find him, we'll let you know."

"I need the photograph," I said, "and I'll find him myself. I thought you might know him. You don't and that's all there is to it. Thanks for everything, Lieutenant, including the rather shallow psychoanalysis of why I carry a gun."

"One more thing, March," he said harshly as I turned to go. "Don't start anything in my district."

"I don't plan on starting anything," I told him. "I do intend to finish a few things. If you're a good boy I might give you the credit for it."

I went out before he could answer. I didn't even look at the Sergeant as I went by. Outside, I climbed into my car. But I noticed that there was a trooper in a car who was making an effort not to look at me. Sure enough, when I pulled out he was right behind me. I smiled. If this kept up I was going to have a parade everywhere I went.

I drove straight back into the village and stopped at the bar. The trooper parked across the street. I went inside. Eddie Sales was working behind the bar and there were five customers. One of them was Nick Potti. I walked down to where he sat.

"How are you today, Nick?" I asked.

"I'm all right," he said. "Where'd you go so early this morning?"

"I went over to call on the state cops. They weren't very friendly. In fact, one of them is outside determined to find out where I go and what I do. I just thought I ought to tell you that you're only going to be part of the crowd from now on."

He repeated his favorite four-letter word. I smiled at him and went to the other end of the bar.

Eddie Sales came over at once. "The usual?" he asked.

"I'm a man of steady habits," I said. "The usual."

He brought the drink and put it in front of me. "He came

in about an hour ago," he said in a low voice. "He didn't ask any questions. He's just been sitting there."

I nodded.

Nick Potti got off of his stool and walked to the front as though he were just looking around. But he was casing the outside. It wasn't hard to spot the police cruiser. Nick came over to me. He looked around the bar. The nearest customer was four stools away.

"Bartender," he said, "I'd like to buy this gentleman a drink."

Eddie Sales came over and poured me a triple V.O. He looked at Nick without any expression. "The gentleman always drinks a triple," he said. "What'll you have?"

"Nothing for me," Nick said harshly. He put two dollars on the bar. "Now beat it. I want to talk to the gentleman." He waited until Eddie had retreated to the other end of the bar. Then he turned to look at me. "What's going on, March? You put the state cops on me?" His voice was low.

"No," I said. "You ought to know better than that, Nick. I play the same rules that you do. It has nothing to do with whether I like you or don't like you. If you think I'm a threat, you'll try to kill me. You get in my way, and I'll kill you. The cops don't like me any better than they like you. He's out there to find out what I'm doing. You already know what I'm doing. I was trying to give you a tip. I don't want the cops to take you—or Jerry. If it has to be done, I'll do my own taking."

"Yeah?" he said, his voice hard.

"Yeah. Let's not kid ourselves, Nick. You know why I'm here. Jerry knows.

Johnny Clark knows. I'm already pretty close. There's not going to be a showdown until I get closer. Then all the talk is going to stop. Now that I'm here, you don't have to stay on my tail all the time. You know my destination better than I do. If you want to stay with me, it's all right. Be my guest. But you're going to collect a man in a uniform on your tail, just as I have. You pays your money and you takes your choice. Or do you have to call Johnny Clark to know what you think? Either way, don't bother me until you're ready to go for the big one." I turned back to my drink.

He hesitated a minute and then went to the other end of the bar. He finished his drink in one gulp and then stalked out.

Eddie Sales came over to me. "How'd you get rid of him?" he asked.

"Told him there was a state cop outside waiting to follow me, and that the path was getting a little crowded. I don't think I got rid of him. He'll still be around. I think he went out now to make a phone call."

"Why is the cop out there?"

"They don't like men who carry guns in their district. We exchanged a few words on the subject, and I think the Lieutenant decided that I should be run out of Orange County if he can only find a reason."

"Do they know you're being followed?"

"No. And now I wouldn't tell them the time of day. Eddie, will you take a look at this?" I brought out the picture. "Ever see this man?"

He looked it over carefully. "He looks familiar," he said uncertainly. "Who is he?"

"A man who disappeared seven years ago. His name was Rako then. He's the one I think is around here somewhere."

"I don't think he's anybody around here," he said slowly. "He looks familiar, but maybe his picture was in the papers and that's the reason."

"Maybe," I said. I took the picture back. I was disappointed. I had hoped it was going to be easy. I should have known that it never is. "Well, I'll see you later."

I went out and got into the Mercury. When I pulled out, the trooper dutifully followed.

I spent the afternoon cruising. I went into Newburgh and bar-hopped for a while, hoping that I might spot Jerry Dell somewhere. But I didn't see him, and there was no sign of Nick Potti. It began to worry me a bit. If I got too close to Rako, Johnny Clark might just decide to take his chances and kill him instead of trying to get me.

When I drew a blank in Newburgh, I tried the bars in New Windsor, Cornwall, and Vails Gate with no better luck. The trooper was my faithful companion throughout.

That night I had dinner in a little Italian restaurant on Route 32. The food was excellent. The trooper had a replacement who waited outside for me. I went back to Eddie's and had a few drinks and then to my motel. I watched television and read, then went to sleep.

The next day was much the same. Only this time, Nick Potti was back on the job. I had breakfast at the same place, stopped in at Eddie's, and went out looking for Jerry Dell again—with the two cars following me. Then suddenly in the middle of the afternoon the trooper left me. I thought that the

Lieutenant must have decided it was costing the taxpayers too much money to have a trooper watch a man who didn't do anything except go to bars. That night I had dinner in a French restaurant—snails and then chicken in wine. I was back at the motel early that night. I was getting nowhere and was disgusted. I was sure that Thomas Rako was somewhere in the neighborhood, but now I was really stuck for leads.

The following morning I went back to the same place in the village for breakfast. Nick Potti was on the job and had coffee while I was eating. The trooper was absent. They must have decided I wasn't worth any more attention. It saddened me.

I didn't go to Eddie's that morning. I started my rounds again right after breakfast. It was pretty much the same story. This time I did manage to find a couple of bookies and I made two bets, but I didn't see anything of Jerry Dell.

I had lunch in one of the Newburgh hotels, and finally, in the middle of the afternoon, I went back to Cornwall-on-Hudson and to Eddie's. He was working behind the bar. He brought over the V.O.

"How's it going?" he asked.

"Lousy," I said. "I have a five spot on Half-a-Doughnut John in the fifth at Aqueduct, another five spot on Jeanne in the seventh, I'm whiskey-logged from pub-crawling, and I don't know a damn bit more than I did when I got here."

"You need to relax," he said. He glanced at the clock on the wall. "We'll take care of it in about twenty minutes. In the meantime you can read the exciting local news. At least we had a murder yesterday." He pulled a newspaper from beneath the bar and tossed it in front of me.

The murder story was on the front page. It wasn't very exciting. There was a picture of a chubby little man with a fierce-looking mustache smiling shyly at his pretty, dark-haired wife. They were the owners of a restaurant on Route 32.

The day before, they'd had a customer who was a stranger. He'd had a lot to drink and stayed on until he was the only customer in the place. He'd pulled a gun and tried to hold them up. Mr. Blake, the restaurant owner, had shot and killed him after the stranger had fired one shot, which missed Blake but shattered the bar mirror.

Blake had been arraigned on a charge of manslaughter and was out on bail. The story left no doubt that he would be freed. It was the last sentence in the story that caught my attention.

"The dead man," the story said, "has been identified as a notorious gangster named Jerry Dell."

TEN

It took a minute before it really registered. It just didn't sound right. Jerry Dell was a professional gunman, and some corn-fed barkeeper had killed him. I took another look at the picture. It was the same. He was still a little fat guy gazing shyly at his wife.

I folded the paper and put it on the bar as Eddie came back. "An interesting story," I said.

"It shows how dangerous it is to run a bar," he said with a smile. "I'm even surprised that Blake had a gun or could use it. He always struck me as a weak sister."

"Well, it doesn't take much strength to pull a trigger," I said. "What do you think'll happen to him?"

"He'll get off. The guy he killed was a known gangster and pulled a gun and shot at him. They'll keep the restaurant and bar closed for a few days until it's settled. That'll be all."

A tall, slender man came in.

"Here's Joe now." Eddie said, nodding at the tall man. "Let's go."

"Where?"

He smiled. "You told me that you've been pub-crawling. Now I'm going to show you where you should have gone."

I finished my drink. "Where are you parked?"

"In the back."

"You go out the front door and I'll go out the back," I said.

"Maybe we can avoid having company if we do that. My friend is parked out there."

"Got it," he said. He came around from behind the bar, putting on a jacket. I got up and walked through the back room and outdoors. A minute later Eddie came around the corner of the building. We climbed into his Rambler and I got down so I couldn't be seen from the outside. Eddie started the car and drove off.

"All right," he said a couple of minutes later. "He stayed where he was and we're out of sight now."

I sat up. "Where are we going?"

"A few places you tourists don't always hit," he said.

"Blake's?"

He glanced at me. "You want to go there, huh?"

"I'd like to."

"We can try it. As I said, he's probably closed. But if he's there, he'll let us in. Why do you want to go there?"

"The man who was killed," I said, "was a friend of the one who's following me. He worked for the same outfit. He was a professional gunman, not a hold-up man, so I'm curious."

"Okay. We'll go there. After we make another stop."

I nodded. "You know Blake?"

"Yes. It's part of the business. Each week I manage to drop into most of the saloons. And the other owners drop into my place. That way you keep up with what's going on. You go into a place, buy a few drinks, do some shop talk, and then go on to another joint."

"A nice racket," I said. "It's all business, so you can take it off your income tax."

"Yeah, but they fight for every dollar of the deduction." We drove through the back roads and he finally pulled into a driveway. There was a sign overhead that identified the place as The Clover Leaf. It was a huge colonial house that must have been the showplace of its day. It was still a handsome building. Around in the back there was a swimming pool and beyond it another, more modern building. It looked like a motel, but there was no sign on it.

"This is the place I'd like to have," Eddie said as he pulled into the parking area. "She's got fifteen rooms in the main house and twenty-five in the other house."

"She?"

"June Murphy. She's not open yet, but she'll let us in."

"How does she do enough business to keep this place going?" I asked as we got out. "She's way out on a back road, and I wouldn't imagine the local people would keep her busy."

"She does a big business during all of the summer season. People from the city coming up for a week or two. And she gets a lot of them for weekends in the spring and fall, right up through the hunting season. That leaves her with three or four slow months, but she still does a fair dinner business then. And she has a few other things that bring in a buck or so."

"What?"

"Well, there's always a couple or three girls around through the summer who are available to male guests and split the take with June. And local groups can come out, buy a jug for ten dollars, and sit on the back porch drinking it and using the pool. She makes out."

"No gambling?" I asked with a smile.

"No. Just the three B's—booze, broads, and bedrooms."

"All essential items," I agreed. "I'm surprised you didn't send me here instead of that motel I'm in."

"You looked like a man who wanted to work, even though you said you were on vacation. You can still move."

We walked up on the wide, sweeping veranda that ran halfway around the house, and Eddie tried the door. It was locked, so he knocked on it. A couple of minutes went by and then somebody peered out of the window before opening the door. We stepped into a large dining room.

"Hi, Eddie," she said. "You never give a girl a chance to get dressed."

"That's the way I like them," he said. "June, meet Milo."

"Hi, Milo," she said.

She was fairly tall, a blonde somewhere in between straw and platinum. My guess was that she was in her forties, but she was well preserved—by nature or Playtex. It was her eyes that made me sure she was older than she looked. She'd had all of her surprises; there weren't going to be any more. And she looked at a man with loving appreciation in the same way a butcher might look at a lamb.

We went through the dining room and into a small, intimate bar. She switched on the lights and went behind the bar. "What'll it be, boys?"

"Scotch for me, V.O. for Milo. Have one with us, June."

She nodded and poured the drinks. She gave herself a brandy and took Eddie's money. "How's business?" she asked.

"Lousy. How about you?"

She shrugged. "You know how it is here. I'm still getting weekenders, but summer is almost here. I had a party out of Newburgh last night—a salesman and a bunch of his customers. I had to drink with them until three." She looked at me. "What do you do, Milo?"

"As little as I can," I said solemnly.

"He's from the city," Eddie volunteered.

She'd been looking me over ever since we came in. Now she glanced at Eddie with a smile. "Is your friend a cop?" she asked. I knew by the way she asked that she'd spotted the gun. So she'd been around.

"Is it necessary to call me a dirty name as soon as you've met me?" I asked.

She laughed. "Sorry. I was just curious about the cut of your jacket."

"I'm a careful man. You know how some people like to have an umbrella with them whenever it rains? Well, I'm like that. I don't like to get wet."

We finished our drinks and she bought a round. She and Eddie talked some more about business and exchanged the latest dirty jokes. Then the phone rang and she went to answer it.

"Let's move on," I said.

"Okay," he said.

We finished our drinks by the time she'd come back. We said good-bye and left. She followed us to the door and made a point of telling me to come back. We got into the car.

"Looks like you made a hit," Eddie said as we pulled out.

"Thanks for nothing," I said. "Where are we going? Blake's?"

"If you want to," he said. He turned and we went back the way we'd come.

"Blake a native son?" I asked.

"No. He came up here sometime after I did. The place was owned by a woman, Carol Shores—a nice-looking broad. Her husband had died a couple of years before that and she'd been running the place by herself. Blake bought a half interest in the place and the next thing we knew they got married. A nice guy, a nice broad—everybody was pleased about it."

"There's nothing like weddings and funerals," I agreed. We drove through the back roads until we finally reached 32 again. Then we turned left toward New Windsor. About a mile down the road Eddie turned in. It was a neat, modern building. The sign said Blake's Inn. There was only one other car parked there. We got out and went over to the entrance. The door was locked. Eddie knocked on it and after a bit he looked out, the man whose picture had been in the paper. He opened the door.

"Hi, Eddie," he said. "I've been closed for a few days, but I guess you and your friend can come in—as long as we keep it quiet."

We followed him inside, through an attractive dining room and into a very pleasant little bar. Eddie and I perched on stools and Blake went behind the bar.

"What'll you have?" he asked.

"Scotch and V.O. on the rocks," Eddie said, "and have one yourself. Tom, this is Milo March. Tom Blake."

We shook hands and he started fixing the drinks. I sat and watched him. Now that I'd seen him full face, I knew he was Thomas Rako. His hair was a little thinner; he had the mustache, and he was maybe twenty-five pounds heavier, but that's who he was.

"Carol's lying down," he said as he brought the drinks. "The last twenty-four hours have been a little rough."

"I was sorry to hear about it," Eddie said. "But you ought to get through it without any trouble. I don't think the ABC can even give you any trouble over it. You had a permit for the gun, didn't you?"

Blake nodded. He kept looking at me and then looking away. But I knew that since he was Rako, he would notice the gun I was carrying sooner or later.

"I guess he spotted the safe," Blake said.

There was a safe in the middle of the bar, down on the floor.

"He must've thought it would be an easy touch and he was drunk. I was lucky." Suddenly his gaze fixed on me and he was no longer the shy, fat man I'd seen in the newspaper picture. "You from around here, March?"

"No," I said. "I'm from the city. You might say this is a sort of vacation."

His gaze had shifted to my left shoulder. "Oh? What do you do when you're not vacationing? Cop?"

"No," Eddie said, "Milo's "

"I'm not a cop," I said quickly. "The pay's too small."

"Who do you work for?" Blake asked.

"Myself," I said. I smiled at him. "You might say I'm a sportsman. I heard that this was a good place to come."

"There's some good shooting around here," he said laconically. "How's business, Eddie?"

"Lousy," Eddie said. "All beer trade. If I could get some-body to give me eleven thousand, I'd sell like a shot. How is it with you?"

"We've been doing pretty good on the dinner trade, but I don't know what this'll do to us."

"You'll be all right," Eddie said. "It might even help."

"Yeah," he said. He was still a little nervous about me, but I was keeping quiet, so he started to relax.

We had one more drink and then left. He was almost cordial as he said good-bye. We went out and got into Eddie's car.

"What was that all about?" he asked as he headed out of the driveway.

"He spotted my gun," I said, "and it made him nervous. Where are you headed now?"

"A couple of places in Newburgh."

"I hate to be a party pooper, but I'd like to go back to your place."

"Okay," he said, and turned the car the other way. We drove back to Cornwall without talking.

"Want to do me a favor?" I asked as we drove down the street to his bar. I could see that Nick Potti was still parked there.

"Sure. What?"

"Drive around in the back where you were parked before. Then trade cars with me for a couple of hours. Mine is that new Mercury there."

"All right," he said.

I slid down to the floor out of sight and we drove in and around to the back. I gave him the keys to the Mercury and he got out. I drove ahead and out the other driveway and took off. I watched the rearview mirror, but Nick Potti stayed where he was. There was no guarantee that he would continue to stay there. I took a roundabout way and went back to my motel. I dug into my suitcase and took out my spare gun. It was a tiny four-shot derringer I'd had a gunsmith make over so that it now fired .32 caliber shells. I checked it and then strapped its holster around my leg, under my trousers, and put the gun in it. I went out again.

I drove down Route 32 until I reached Blake's Inn and pulled in. I walked over and knocked on the door. I saw him looking out the window and then he opened the door about an inch.

"I'm sorry," he said. "I told you that I'm supposed to be closed. The only reason I let you in before was because Eddie's a friend of mine."

I put my foot in the door before he could close it. "I'm the reason," I said, "that Jerry Dell tried to kill you. You'd better let me come in and talk to you."

Suddenly he looked tired. He opened the door and I stepped inside. I followed him into the bar.

"A drink?" he asked automatically.

"No, I've had enough for the time," I said.

He'd taken a cloth and was rubbing the top of the bar as though he didn't know what he was doing. "I thought you said you wasn't a cop," he said.

"I'm not. I work for an insurance company. We have to pay a million dollars the day you're declared legally dead. That's a lot of money. We don't like to lose it."

"I don't have any insurance," he said. He was making a last stand, but his heart wasn't in it.

"Tom Blake may not, but Tom Rako does. You know better than that. Johnny Clark can send a hundred Jerry Dells—and he will if he has to. He's obviously made a decision about you."

"What do you mean?"

"Jerry Dell tried to kill you, didn't he? So Johnny Clark must have decided that he'd rather take a chance on fighting the evidence you might leave behind than the testimony of a live witness."

He stared at me dully. "How did you find me, March?"

"Partly luck, partly figuring out what you must have done, and partly Johnny Clark's stupidity."

"You think you're going to take me back?" he asked.

I shook my head. "I wouldn't think of it. I'm not interested in taking you anywhere. I've discovered that you're still alive and that's all I was interested in doing. Of course, the situation may change any minute."

"What does that mean?"

"If you're smart, Rako, you'll take yourself back."

"Why?"

"I can think of two reasons. You won't be facing very much. Contempt of Congress is only one year if you get sent up. You can probably bargain your way out of that by telling what you know about Johnny Clark. You might even be able to make a deal on the bigamy charge. None of those are as serious as the alternative."

"What's that?"

"You already know the answer to that. Johnny Clark sent Jerry Dell to kill you if I got too close. So you got Jerry, but do you think it's going to end there? Nick Potti is already in the neighborhood. Maybe you can kill him. Clark will send another one and another one and another one until somebody gets you."

"I'm going to call Johnny. He'll see it my way."

"Not anymore. Sure, he's seen it your way for almost seven years, but now he's more afraid of you than he is of what you have. And he'll see that there's no turning back now that I've found you."

"I could kill you," he said. His hands were out of sight under the bar. "That would show Johnny I was on the level."

"You can try," I said gently, "but I don't think you'll make it." My hand was already on my gun beneath my coat.

"We can work something out," he said desperately. "I'm supposed to get half of that million dollars when the court declares me dead. Johnny gets the other half. I'll split my half with you. I've already put the restaurant up for sale. We're going to Brazil as soon as I get the half million."

"And your evidence against Johnny?"

"He gets it back as soon as I get to Brazil. That's the agreement."

I shook my head. "You can't buy me, Rako, but that's not even the point. Johnny Clark is no longer going to let you live to collect your half million. He doesn't dare let you live."

"He has to. It must have been some kind of mistake with Jerry Dell. All I have to do is talk to Johnny."

"You killed Dell yesterday. Why haven't you talked to Johnny already?"

"I've called three times but he wasn't in."

"He's not going to be in to you. Get smart, Rako. Johnny Clark has become a lot more successful and powerful since you were around him. He's decided that he can take a chance on whatever you've got on him, but that he can't take a chance on you."

He had a trapped look. "He has to take a chance on me. I could send him up for murder."

"Maybe. I don't know what evidence you have, but he might very well beat it if you weren't around to testify. He's probably already talked to his lawyers and knows where he stands."

"But I've got the evidence. I've got the gun he used to kill a man ten years ago—with his prints all over it. He told me to dump it, but I put it away for insurance."

"I think your policy just ran out," I told him. "With you dead, Johnny Clark could probably beat that with no trouble."

"I've made an affidavit about what I saw."

"He might beat that, too, providing the authorities ever get it. His hired killer might find it—in your safe there, for example. And besides, you'd be dead, very dead."

He stared at me like a cornered animal. "You're not going to take me in. You have no authority."

"I'm not even going to try to take you anywhere," I said.

"Then what do you want from me?"

"I don't want anything from you, Rako. If you're smart, I think you'll walk out of here and go with me to the State Police. They'll take you into custody and see that nobody shoots you. That sounds to me like the best offer you have.

By the way, how did you get the best of Jerry Dell? He was supposed to be pretty good."

"I had a gun under the bar," he said dully. "He told me to open the safe. I took the gun with me when I turned to do it. I opened the safe and when I turned back I had the gun on him. He was looking at the safe. I shot him. His gun went off as he fell, and hit back there." He gestured behind him to where the lower corner of the mirror was cracked.

"The affidavit in the safe?" I asked.

"It's there, but the gun's in a safe-deposit box in Newburgh. Why can't you just walk away and leave me alone, March?"

"I could leave you alone," I told him, "but Johnny Clark isn't going to, not any longer."

He shook his head as though he couldn't understand.

"If nobody had found you during the next month," I said, "he might have let you go to Brazil, but I have an idea that something would have happened to you there. Since you have been found, Johnny Clark can't afford to let you stay alive. You were in the business long enough, Rako. You should know that."

"If I could talk to Johnny …"

"Go ahead and try again," I said.

There was a knock on the front door. Rako looked startled for a minute, then his face smoothed out. The knock was repeated.

"I was supposed to get a liquor delivery today," he said. "That must be it now. I'll go let him in." He looked at me questioningly.

"Go ahead," I said. "Get it straight, Rako. I'm not here to

threaten you in any way. I'm here to try to save your life. So go ahead and let in your whiskey."

He brought his hands into sight and walked out from behind the bar. He looked at me for a minute, then walked heavily into the dining room toward the front door. I lit a cigarette and waited. I could hear the faint murmur of voices and then the sound of footsteps coming closer. The minute I saw Rako's face I knew I'd made a mistake, but it was too late. Nick Potti was right behind him with a gun in his hand.

"Relax, March," he said. He finally looked happy. "I guess you thought that was a pretty smart trick, trading cars with the clown in the bar."

Rako had started to go behind the bar.

"Uh-uh," Nick said, prodding him with the gun. "That's where you were when you shot Jerry. Maybe you got another gun there. Get over to the wall. You, too, March."

I slid off the stool and backed over to the wall. Rako was beside me. His face was pale. I guess he finally realized I'd been right.

"Both of you turn around and put your hands up on the wall. Lean your weight on them."

We both obeyed. Nick Potti came over and took my gun. He patted my coat and pants pockets, then turned his attention to Rako. When he'd finished, he went back across the room.

"All right," he said. "You can both go over and sit on the bar stools. But move nice and easy so I don't get nervous."

He waited until we were both seated. Then he smiled at Rako. "Hi, Tom. Long time no see."

"I didn't get a chance to tell you that I was glad to see you, Nick," Rako said. He was going to make a last pathetic try, but it was too obvious. "This fellow was just going to take me in to the cops."

"Sure," Nick said soothingly. "We wouldn't want that to happen, would we, Tom boy? We don't like cops, do we?"

"That's right, Nick," he said eagerly.

"And bright boy over there is a sort of cop, too. We don't like him either. Isn't that right, Tom?"

"Sure, Nick."

"That's right, Nick, sure, Nick," he mocked. "You've changed, Tom boy. You used to be a real snotty little bastard. Thought you were a big man. Now you talk real quiet. You've got fat and you've got a nice business here. I even hear you're shacked up with a good-looking broad. Where is she?"

"Upstairs, asleep." Rako's voice had changed as if he'd finally realized that nothing was going to help.

"That's nice. When I'm through with you two, maybe I'll go up and give her a good time."

Rako's face tightened and turned paler. He started to say something, then clamped his mouth shut.

"I guess you're still feeling big," Nick said. "You killed Jerry Dell, and he was a hard man to kill. You even fixed it so you'll probably get off with a suspended sentence. Smart. Maybe too smart. It would've solved all our problems if you'd arranged it so you could go to the chair."

Rako stared at him silently.

"You're both awful quiet," Nick said mockingly. "Bright boy, there, has been so smart he doesn't know when his luck runs out. And tough Tommy—killer Rako—he's got nothing to say either, when the gun's on the other end."

"I notice you talk a little tougher when you're holding a gun," I said.

"Sure I do, bright boy. And I'm going to keep talking like that as long as you can hear."

"Maybe."

"Shut up," he said. "I've got some talking to do, Tom boy. Johnny says you have a couple of things that belong to him. He wants them."

Rako pursed his lips tighter and said nothing.

"And he's going to get them, ain't he, Tom boy? You know how good Johnny's been to you. You're not going to try to keep him from having what belongs to him."

"I don't know what you're talking about," Rako said tightly.

"Sure you do, Tom. I'm talking about a piece of paper and a gun, that's all. You got them in that little dinky safe there?"

Rako was silent for a minute, then his lips moved stiffly. "The paper is here, but the gun is in a safe-deposit box in a bank and you can't get that. My lawyer has my will, which says that the box is to be turned over to the cops if anything happens to me."

"Now, that was pretty smart," Nick said. "I didn't think you had it in you, Tom boy. But I think we can maybe solve that problem, don't you?"

"What do you mean?"

"I think it can be worked out," Nick said. "Everything can be. It's no secret that March has been looking for you. So he found you and you decided to shoot it out. This time both of you lost. You get killed by March's gun and he gets killed by yours. I'm sure you have one back there somewhere. Neat, huh?"

"The cops will still get the gun that's in the safe-deposit box."

"I have a couple of ideas about that, too. I can put March on ice and you can go get the gun while I stay here with your broad. I think I like that one the best."

"What's the other idea?"

"Well, the three of us can stay here like three pals, and your wife—is that what you call her?—can go get the gun. Only she has to understand that if she makes a false move, you're out like a light."

"I'm going to be anyway," Rako said.

"Sure, but there's always hope, isn't there? Bright boy might try to be a hero. The cops might just happen to stop in to see if your liquor license is okay. A lot of things could happen, Tom boy. As long as you're alive, things are great."

"All right," Rako said. "She'll go. I'll go get her."

"Uh-uh. We'll all three go get her. It's always nice to see a broad when she first wakes up. Even March might like it. What kind of nightgown does she wear? Or does she sleep in the raw?"

Rako's voice was a mere croak when he answered. "We don't have to go up. There's an intercom back of the bar. I can call her on that."

"Don't be in a hurry, Tom boy. We'll take care of it in a minute. First let's see if there's a gun back there." He dropped my gun in his pocket and moved around behind the bar. "Everybody sit nice and quiet, just like you were in Sunday School. Yeah, there it is. I'm glad you didn't disappoint me, Tom boy. I remembered that you were always careful enough to have a spare gun somewhere around. While I'm here, would anybody like a drink? On the house. It may be the last drink that Tom ever buys."

When he'd gone behind the bar I'd reached down and taken the derringer from its holster. I held it beside my leg and swung around on the stool. I thought Rako saw me take it out, but he didn't let on. He swung around, too.

"Sure," I said. "I never turn down a free drink."

"Cool, ain't you?" Nick said. "You think it's one of them Indian movies where the cavalry's going to come galloping in at the last minute. Are you going to be surprised."

He put Rako's gun in his other pocket and picked up a glass with his left hand. He put it down in front of me and reached for a bottle.

"Since it's free, it won't make much difference what it is." He splashed whiskey into the glass and put the bottle down. He got two more glasses and poured liquid into them. "To you, Tom boy," he said. "May you have a good time in hell with Jerry." He tossed off his drink and started around the end of the bar. "You can call the broad now."

I was waiting for him when he came into full view. I had the derringer steadied on my knee and there was just enough time to make it a good shot. I hit him right in the kneecap. He went down, screaming with pain, his own gun falling from his hand. He rolled around on the floor and then reached for the gun. I shot again, putting a bullet through his hand. He screamed again and fainted.

I walked over and took the three guns. I looked up at Rako.

"Where do you stand now?" I asked.

"I'll go with you," he said. There was no expression on his face.

"Get me a couple of towels."

He went behind the bar and came back with two towels. He handed them to me.

Nick's leg was bleeding badly. I tied one towel tightly around the leg above the knee. His hand wasn't bleeding so much, but even so I wrapped the other towel around it. I had just finished when I heard a clatter of feet. A pretty little brunette, wearing a dressing gown, came rushing into the room.

"Tom," she cried, "what is it?"

"It's all right, honey," he said. "Another man came in and tried to get rough, but Mr. March here took care of it. I'm going to go with Mr. March to take him to the police. I'll tell you about it later." He looked at me almost defiantly. "Mr. March, this is my wife."

"Hello, Mrs. Blake," I said. "I'm sorry about this, but your husband is all right—and I think he's going to be all right from here on in."

"I don't understand," she said, looking from one of us to the other.

"I'll explain it to you later, honey," he said, patting her shoulder. "Now we have to get this man to the police so he can get some medical care."

We carried Nick Potti out and put him in the back seat of Eddie's car. Then we both got into the car and I started the motor.

"Thanks, March," Rako said.

"You're welcome. But you're still going to have to explain it to her."

"I know," he said.

We drove all the way to the State Police barracks on 9-W without talking. Nick Potti was still unconscious when we got there. We left him in the back of the car and went in. The same sergeant was on duty.

"Lieutenant Pilus, please," I said.

He gave me a sour glance but picked up the phone. "That man March is back again," he said. "There's another guy with him. He wants to see you." He listened a minute and then hung up. "You can go in."

"Thank you, Sergeant. Oh, by the way, I have a Rambler parked outside. There's a man in the back seat who's rather badly wounded. You might take care of him. Then you can book him for attempted murder. We're both witnesses. And I shot him—if you're curious about that." I didn't wait for an answer. I went on back to the Lieutenant's office, with Rako following me. I opened the door and went in.

The Lieutenant looked up. "What is it now, March?" he asked sharply.

"Not much," I said. "Do you know this man with me?" His gaze shifted to Rako.

"Certainly. He's Thomas Blake and he runs a restaurant on Route 32. He's the one who killed a hold-up man yesterday. What about it?"

"His real name," I said, "is Thomas Rako. He disappeared from Washington seven years ago after pleading the Fifth about a hundred times before a Congressional hearing. The man he shot yesterday was a professional gunman who was sent here to kill him. There's another one outside in my car who tried the same thing today. I shot that one, but he's still alive."

The Lieutenant stared at me with his mouth open. "Are you telling me that there's a wounded man outside in your car?"

"I think he is. I told your sergeant, so by this time he may be in the building. I imagine the Sergeant is competent enough for that."

The Lieutenant's face was a pale purple. "I suppose you shot him with that gun you have a permit for?"

"Not the one you know about. I shot him with a derringer that's been adapted to use a .32 shell. I have a permit for it, too. In the meantime Mr. Rako has some things he'd like to tell you, and I assure you that Washington will be very interested, much more than in what kind of gun I used. You're likely to end up being a big man, Lieutenant. I'll see you later."

"Just a minute," he said. "You can't go around shooting people, delivering the body here, and then walking out."

"Can't I?" I asked. "Lieutenant, I shot and wounded a man this afternoon. He is a known criminal named Nick Potti from Cleveland, Ohio. I did it to keep him from killing Mr. Rako and myself. I have a permit for the gun that was used. I have a perfectly legal license from the state of New York to operate as a private detective anywhere within the state. In the meantime, you have a much more important story to get from Mr. Rako. I'm staying at the George Washington Motel in Cornwall. I'll be available for any hearing that's held. I'm fully bonded and responsible. I'm also tired. I'm going back to the motel to go to sleep in spite of the fact that it's very early. Is that perfectly clear?"

"I could arrest you," he said angrily.

"Sure, you could. You could also start looking like a monkey when the newspapers started checking into it. They'll make quite a story out of the fact that Rako has been here right under your nose for seven years."

"Are you trying to blackmail me into letting you go?"

"I wouldn't try to blackmail you into giving me the time of day. I'm just trying to keep you from being a bigger fool than nature made you. Incidentally," I added, reaching into my pockets, "here's the gun Nick Potti was carrying, here's a spare gun that Rako had, and here's the gun I shot Potti with. I want a receipt for it."

He grabbed a sheet of paper and scribbled on it, then signed his name.

"I'll remain in town until after the hearing." I looked at Rako. "You'll be all right now, Rako. You can stop running and Johnny can start. I'll see you around, Lieutenant."

"You'd better," he said grimly.

I went out. Nick Potti was sitting in the front office; the Sergeant was still patching him up.

"Why don't you get him a doctor?" I asked. "Or would that strain the state budget too much?"

"There's an ambulance coming for him. You shattered his kneecap."

"I know. That was the general idea. I trust that when he goes to the hospital it will be under arrest."

"He will be." He looked up. "Why aren't you?"

"Because I'm a law-abiding citizen, Sergeant," I said, giving him my best smile. "So long, Nick. I'll give Johnny your regards."

His face was contorted with pain and anger as I went out.

ELEVEN

I got into the Rambler and drove back to the bar in Cornwall. I went inside and traded car keys with Eddie. He put a drink in front of me. I hadn't intended having one, but once it was there, I changed my mind.

"Your friend came in and discovered you weren't here," he said.

"I know."

"Anything happen?" he asked.

I finished my drink. "I'll tell you later, Eddie. Now I'm going to get some sleep."

I left and drove the Mercury to the motel. I went in, stripping off my coat and tie. I stretched out on the bed and went to sleep at once.

When I woke up, it was almost midnight. I felt much better. I got up and washed my face in cold water. I put on my tie and coat and went out to the Mercury. I drove into Newburgh and cruised around until I finally found a place that looked like a nightclub. I parked and went in.

It wasn't any Stork Club, but it wasn't too bad. I went to the bar and had a drink. At least the prices were what they should be in a nightclub. I ordered a second one and got a lot of change from the bartender. I called George Macklin in Washington and gave him his story. Then I gave the operator

Martin Raymond's home phone number.

He answered on the third ring. His voice didn't sound sleepy. I was disappointed.

"Milo March," I told him.

"Milo," he said, "Where are you?"

"In Newburgh, New York, spending your money in a high-priced gin mill."

He laughed, but his heart wasn't in it. "What in the world are you doing there?"

"I already told you. I thought you'd sleep better if you knew you'd saved your million dollars."

"You found Rako?"

"I found him. He's now with the New York State Police. And I seem to recall that something was said about a bonus."

"You'll get it, my boy. This is the best news I've had in years. The Board will be delighted."

"I'm delighted that the Board will be delighted. I have to stay here a few days, at your expense, of course, until after a hearing. I shot someone, and they always like to ask questions."

"Not Rako, I hope," he said with alarm.

"Would I endanger your million dollars like that?" I asked. "Good night, Martin."

I hung up and put another dime in the phone. I gave the operator another number in New York and put in more change. When a man answered, I could hear music and the rumble of voices in the background.

"Harry?" I asked.

"Yeah. Who's this?"

"Milo March. Did that canary ever show up?"

"Did she ever?" he said. "She opened tonight and she's strictly from Hitsville. Milo, I could kiss you."

"Please," I said. "I have a delicate stomach and you're not my type. Can I talk to her?"

"Sure, but why don't you come on down? You can catch her last show."

"I'm sixty miles away, Harry, and it's too long a walk. I'm very fond of all the Kennedys, but I don't go for this fifty-mile hike bit."*

"I'll get her," he said.

I waited and then her voice came on. "Hi," she said. She sounded excited.

"Hi, honey," I said. "How's it going?"

"Oh, Milo, it's wonderful. I was scared to death, but everybody's been so wonderful. Where are you?"

"Upstate. I just finished working and I thought I'd see if you were there. You didn't have any trouble leaving Cleveland?"

"No. Nick Potti suddenly left town last week, and I left the day after he did. I don't know where he went."

"He's up here," I said. "At the moment he's in the hospital with a bullet through his knee and another one through his hand."

"Oh?" she said. "Are you all right?"

"I'm fine," I said, "except that I have to stay here for a few days. I'm glad you're a hit, honey. I'll be in the city in two or three days and we'll celebrate."

---

* Attorney General Robert F. Kennedy helped make hiking and fitness extremely popular after he completed a fifty-mile hike in one day in 1963, on a challenge from his brother, President John Kennedy.

"Hurry up, Milo," she said.

I said good-bye and hung up. I went out and had my drink, then two more. I got into the Mercury and drove to Cornwall. Eddie's place was closed. So was everything else. It was just as well. I drove out to the motel and went back to sleep.

Kendell Foster Crossen (1910–1981), the only child of Samuel Richard Crossen and Clo Foster Crossen, was born on a farm outside Albany in Athens County, Ohio—a village of some 550 souls in the year of this birth. His ancestors on his mother's side include the 19th-century songwriter Stephen Collins Foster ("Oh! Susanna"); William

Allen, founder of Allentown, Pennsylvania; and Ebenezer Foster, one of the Minute Men who sprang to arms at the Lexington alarm in April 1775.

Ken went to Rio Grande College on a football scholarship but stayed only one year. "When I was fairly young, I developed the disgusting habit of reading," says Milo March, and it seems Ken Crossen, too, preferred self-education. He loved literature and poetry; favorite authors included Christopher Marlowe and Robert Service. He also enjoyed participant sports and was a semi-pro fighter in the heavyweight class. He became a practicing magician and had a passion for chess.

After college Ken wrote several one-act plays that were produced in a small Cleveland theater. He worked in steel mills and Fisher Body plants. Then he was employed as an insurance investigator, or "claims adjuster," in Cleveland. But he left the job and returned to the theater, now as a performer: a tumbling clown in the Tom Mix Circus; a comic and carnival barker for a tent show, and an actor in a medicine show.

In 1935, Ken hitchhiked to New York City with a typewriter under his arm, and found work with the WPA Writers' Project, covering cricket for the *New York City Guidebook*. In 1936, he was hired by the Munsey Publishing Company as associate editor of the popular *Detective Fiction Weekly*. The company asked him to come up with a character to compete with The Shadow, and thus was born a unique superhero of pulps, comic books, and radio—The Green Lama, an American mystic trained in Tibetan Buddhism.

Crossen sold his first story, "The Aaron Burr Murder Case," to *Detective Fiction Weekly* in September 1939, but says he didn't begin to make a living from writing till 1941. He tried his hand at publishing true crime magazines, comics, and a picture magazine, without great success, so he set out for Hollywood. From his typewriter flowed hundreds of stories, short novels for magazines, scripts radio, television, and film, nonfiction articles. He delved into science fiction in the 1950s, starting with "Restricted Clientele" (February 1951). His dystopian novels *Year of Consent* and *The Rest Must Die* also appeared in this decade.

In the course of his career Ken Crossen acquired six pseud-onyms: Richard Foster, Bennett Barlay, Kent Richards, Clay Richards, Christopher Monig, and M.E. Chaber. The variety was necessary because different publishers wanted to reserve specific bylines for their own publications. Ken based "M.E. Chaber" on the Hebrew word for "author," *mechaber*.

In the early '50s, as M.E. Chaber, Crossen began to write a series of full-length mystery/espionage novels featuring Milo March, an insurance investigator. The first, *Hangman's Harvest*, was published in 1952. In all, there are twenty-two Milo March novels. One, *The Man Inside*, was made into a British film starring Jack Palance.

Most of Ken's characters were private detectives, and Milo was the most popular. Paperback Library reissued twenty-five Crossen titles in 1970–1971, with covers by Robert McGin-nis. Twenty were Milo March novels, four featured an insur-ance investigator named Brian Brett, and one was about CIA agent Kim Locke.

Crossen excelled at producing well-plotted entertainment with fast-moving action. His research skills were a strong asset, back when research meant long hours searching library microfilms and poring over street maps and hotel floorplans. His imagination took him to many international hot spots, although he himself never traveled abroad. Like Milo March, he hated flying ("When you've seen one cloud, you've seen them all").

Ken Crossen was married four times. With his first wife he had three children (Stephen, Karen, Kendra) and with his second a son (David). He lived in New York, Florida, Southern California, Nevada, and other parts of the country. Milo March moves from Denver to New York City after five books of the series, with an apartment on Perry Street in Greenwich Village; that's where Ken lived, too. His and Milo's favorite watering hole was the Blue Mill Tavern, a short walk from the apartment.

Ken Crossen was a combination of many of the traits of his different male characters: tough, adventuresome, with a taste for gin and shapely women. But perhaps the best observation was made in an obituary written by sci-fi writer Avram David-son, who described Ken as a fundamentally gentle person who had been buffeted by many winds.

www.ingramcontent.com/pod-product-compliance
Lightning Source LLC
Chambersburg PA
CBHW020607250626
47154CB00004B/1396